———————— ★ ————————

Danny ran the length of the platform and could hear his pursuer sprinting toward him. Danny's heart thumped, his chest heaving, as he glanced everywhere, looking for a way out.

"You!" The guy in the turtleneck shouted as he approached, his face flushed and beaded with sweat.

A couple standing near Danny moved away as if expecting trouble. He still looked around desperately for a way out, but faced the solid wall of the underground station. He strained to see down the track, praying a train would come.

"We need to talk," the guy said as he came within six feet. Something flashed in his hand. A knife? A gun?

Just then Danny saw the headlight of the uptown train in the tunnel across the tracks. The man was close enough to touch him now, and he reached out his right hand and pointed a gun at Danny's stomach. A Claddagh ring—two hands cradling a heart with a crown—glittered on his index finger, which rested against the trigger.

Before he had time to think about the danger, Danny leapt onto the tracks.

———————— ★ ————————

"...engaging and well-plotted mystery. Recommended."
—*I Love A Mystery*

Previously published Worldwide Mystery titles by
JONATHAN HARRINGTON

THE DEATH OF COUSIN ROSE
THE SECOND SORROWFUL MYSTERY

Jonathan Harrington

A Great Day for Dying

W🌐RLDWIDE®

TORONTO • NEW YORK • LONDON
AMSTERDAM • PARIS • SYDNEY • HAMBURG
STOCKHOLM • ATHENS • TOKYO • MILAN
MADRID • WARSAW • BUDAPEST • AUCKLAND

A GREAT DAY FOR DYING

A Worldwide Mystery/March 2002

First published by Write Way Publishing, Inc.

ISBN 0-373-26413-5

Printed in U.S.A.

To my brothers and sister,
from whom I learned
the pleasure
of a
good story.

Pour a glass.
Pull up a chair.
This story is for you.

ONE

"St. Patrick's Day is about the wearing of the *green*," Fintan Conway yelled at a young reporter from *Out Loud!*, who stood along the wall midway to the podium, "not the wearing of the *pink!*" The hapless reporter had asked Conway, grand marshal of the St. Patrick's Day Parade, why GILA—the Gay Irish & Lesbian Alliance—had been denied a place in the line of march for the tenth year in a row.

"You bigot," a middle-aged woman near the back of the room shouted at Conway, and at least a quarter of the people in the room burst into applause.

The grand marshal smiled and leaned into the microphone. Fintan Conway was of middle weight, dressed in a neat gray suit and white tie printed with green shamrocks. He had shaggy silver hair, a bushy silver mustache, and eyebrows set off by a face so bright red it glowed. A white, green, and orange grand marshal sash was draped over his right shoulder and across his chest. His blue eyes gleamed in the soft roundness of his flushed face and he smirked as if remembering some vulgar joke. Although he was a journalist himself, he looked down from the podium with disdain at the media gathered for his St. Patrick's Day message.

"You have a question?" he asked a young woman

in a trim business suit, her reporter's notebook open on her lap.

"I want a response to my question," shouted the reporter from *Out Loud!*

"You got your response."

"Well, it's unacceptable."

"Accept it, kid." Conway loved confrontation and the more emotions boiled over at the press conference, the more skillfully he could manipulate the crowd's anger. "And shut up. Yes?"

The room was peppered with boos.

"I'm Sheila McNamara of the *Irish Echo.*"

"I know who you are, Sheila. Nice suit."

The young woman, flustered by the sexist remark, looked down at her notes and dropped her pen. When she bent to pick it up she dropped her notebook.

"See if you can remember the question without your notes, Sheila."

The reporter stood up, eyes blazing. "You wrote in a recent column that you fully support implementation of the executive power-sharing clause of the Good Friday Agreement signed by all parties to the Northern Ireland conflict."

"Very good, Sheila. What's your question?"

"Yet you also wrote that decommissioning by the IRA will never happen. Will you explain that remark?"

"The IRA is nothing but a bunch of thugs who murder innocent people and blow the kneecaps off their own kind. You think they're going to destroy their weapons voluntarily?"

Now the hot, airless room exploded into shouts and booing. "You traitor," someone yelled over the catcalls.

Fintan Conway rocked back on his heels and gave the crowd of shouting reporters, TV personnel, and the pre-parade citizens gathered for the press conference his most generous smile.

Most people standing at the front of a stuffy room crowded with men and women screaming insults would be intimidated. Or at least show some sign of distress. Not Fintan Conway. The grand marshal was in his element and he beamed with satisfaction.

"And the Loyalist paramilitary groups are even worse," he added. "They're the scum of the earth."

As quickly as the booing had begun, Conway had turned it into shouts of approval and applause. "So you've got thugs promising scum that they'll all put down their guns, shake hands, and live happily ever after. Do you really believe that fairy tale, Sheila?"

Donald Boyle, the chairman of the NYC St. Patrick's Day Parade and Celebration Committee, sat on a metal folding chair beside the podium next to another elderly member of the Ancient Order of Hibernians. Boyle had opposed Fintan Conway's appointment as grand marshal from the beginning.

"He's a public relations nightmare," Boyle whispered to his colleague beside him. "No grand marshal in history has ever insulted the IRA."

His elderly colleague whispered back, "Sure, he might damage the image of the parade beyond repair."

Conway had already alienated almost every segment of the Irish community. He had insulted the mayor at the traditional breakfast that morning. Later he refused to shake hands with Cardinal Edward Egan, the new archbishop of New York, after Mass at St. Patrick's Cathedral. Cardinal Egan had replaced John Cardinal O'Connor the year before.

Now just ten minutes into his press conference, Fintan Conway had turned what was traditionally a feel-good PR session for the public and the press into a broiling inferno. Worst of all, Conway seemed to be enjoying every minute of it.

"You call yourself a Roman Catholic, yet you openly oppose the fundamental teaching of the Church on human life," began a middle-aged man in a Roman collar who was a reporter for *The Catholic Nation* as well as a Jesuit priest. "You've published numerous columns attacking the Right-to-Life Movement and advocating *more* liberal abortion laws. Explain yourself."

"You explain *yourself*, Father," Conway shot back. "Are you planning to get pregnant any time soon? Will you ever have to make the difficult choice to have an abortion or not? The answer is no, you won't. You never have to face that decision yourself. Neither will any of the other *men* who make up seventy-seven percent of the leadership of the anti-abortion mafia. So if you don't have to face the choice yourself, why not just mind your own business?"

"This is outrageous," the elderly AOH member whispered to Boyle.

Fintan Conway mugged for the TV cameras.

Don Boyle nodded. "It's all too political. Why isn't he talking about Irish pride, about the contribution of the Irish to America, about the way we pulled ourselves up by the bootstraps? Ourselves alone!"

Conway recognized another reporter. "You in the back there."

A young male correspondent for the *Irish Voice*

rose. "I'm sure you're aware that deposits of gold have been discovered on Croagh Patrick, the holy mountain in County Mayo, Ireland. Environmentalists oppose any development in the area, yet the Church has given its tacit approval for exploration and mining. You were born in Mayo. Any thoughts on the subject? After all, it is St. Patrick's Day and this is St. Patrick's mountain."

"I certainly do have thoughts and I thank you for an intelligent question, at last. Yes, I was born and raised at the foot of that mountain. I still own property there. And by the way, I'll have a lot more to say on this subject in my column next week. But for now let me tell you I think it's a travesty that the leadership of the Church is permitting the desecration of a holy pilgrimage site for profit."

The reporter from *The Catholic Nation* was on his feet. "That's unfair."

"Oh, sit down, Father, before you have a heart attack."

In fact, the priest did look as though he might have a coronary as he fell back into his chair.

Don Boyle took a handkerchief from his coat pocket and mopped his brow. The temperature in the room seemed to be rising along with the tempers of the crowd. "The media is going to crucify us after this," he whispered to his colleague. "Make all the Irish in the city look bad. Why doesn't he just shut up and sit down?"

"You express a pro-choice point of view in your newspaper columns," another reporter put in, "yet you've written numerous columns in opposition to euthanasia or even removing terminal patients from life support. That seems contradictory."

"Does it? I don't want anybody pulling my plug," said Conway. "If the doctors can eliminate the terminally ill, who's next? The elderly? The disabled? The handicapped?"

"That's absurd."

"Ideological BS," someone else shouted.

"Any time you question the medical mafia," Conway shouted back, "you're faced with criticism."

"What in God's name does any of this have to do with St. Patrick's Day?" Don Boyle asked out of the corner of his mouth. He forced a smile for the camera crews and fidgeted with the notes of his own statement. "Something has to be done before Conway ruins St. Paddy's Day completely."

Boyle labored to his feet, gently pushed Conway aside, and leaned into the microphone. "I'm sure the grand marshal would like to say a few words now about today's parade," he said. "How about a word of thanks to all the wonderful people of New York where—at least for today—everyone is Irish."

Fintan Conway shot Boyle a look, then gazed through the brightness of the television lights and sneered. "Sure, it's a great day for the Irish," he sang in an exaggerated brogue, "it's a great day for the fair." He skipped around behind the microphone as he sang the old song. "Is this what you want, Don? Shamrocks and leprechauns?"

Don Boyle dropped back heavily into his chair and kneaded his forehead with both hands. "I can't believe this is happening," he muttered. "He's up there singing. How many mimosas did Finn drink at the breakfast meeting this morning? That idiot is singing and dancing a jig in front of hundreds of reporters and television cameras. He's acting out every negative stereotype of the Irish it has taken us a century to destroy.''

"The sidewalks of New York are thick with blarney..." Conway sang off pitch.

"This is worse than I even imagined," Boyle went on as if talking to himself. "Doesn't he have any self-respect at all?''

Fintan Conway abruptly stopped his clowning and faced the reporters and camera crews. "Seriously folks, it is a great day for the Irish and I'm honored to have been chosen as grand marshal of this year's parade.''

"Did he say *chosen?*" Boyle snorted. "That idiot bulldozed his way into the post. Nobody in his right mind would have chosen him as grand marshal. Why in God's name did it have to happen on our watch?''

"There are a lot of people working behind the scenes to make this parade happen," Conway continued, "all too numerous to mention."

"Yeah, why bother," Boyle said wearily. "It might take the spotlight off you for a second.''

Conway put his hand over his heart in mock reverence and his eyes twinkled with crocodile tears. "May the road rise up to meet you. May the wind be always at your back..." he stammered, pretending to forget his lines. "Oh, yeah. And may you be in heaven half an hour before the devil knows you're dead!''

TWO

"HAVE YOU HEARD Brendan's in town?"

Fidelma Muldoon swept her blazing red mane away from her face and turned her green eyes to Danny O'Flaherty who stood beside her on the crowded sidewalk in front of the Sherry-Netherland Hotel at 5th Avenue and Central Park South in Manhattan. Fidelma's fair skin and glowing cherry cheeks, combined with the thick layers of her curly red hair, made it seem as though her brilliant smile might suddenly burst into flames.

"Brendan Grady?" Danny asked.

Fidelma dressed less formally since moving to New York. She wore spandex leggings that accentuated her shapely thighs, and a bright red silk blouse that she would never have worn back in her hometown of Ballycara, Ireland, where she had worked as the sacristan for the parish. After the priest's death she had moved to Dublin, where she worked briefly in the Office of the Chancery of the Catholic Church. Then she had come on a three-month tourist visa to New York and found work—albeit illegally—as a nanny for a family in Yorkville on Manhattan's East Side, and was still here beyond the limits of her visa.

She had dragged Danny to Cardinal Egan's early

morning Mass at St. Patrick's Cathedral that morning. Over four thousand people had heard the new Archbishop of New York celebrate Mass in the 2,500-seat cathedral. Danny had reluctantly agreed to go with Fidelma to Mass, then to the St. Patrick's Day parade.

But he had refused to go to the grand marshal's press conference. Fidelma's roommate worked for the *Irish Echo* and she had gone with her instead. Fidelma recounted the circus of the press conference. "What a horrible man!" she had said of Conway. "I thought the grand marshal was supposed to be a unifying figure that all the Irish could look to with pride?"

Danny's only comment had been: "Fintan Conway's a loose cannon."

As for the parade, Danny wasn't fond of the bogus Irish atmosphere of green plastic bowler hats and day-glow shamrocks. But Fidelma was anxious to see what St. Patrick's Day in New York was all about.

"Brendan Grady's in the States?" Danny asked.

"That's right," Fidelma said. "Here in Manhattan."

It was almost 60 degrees. The sun illuminated the glass and chrome spires of Midtown and they gleamed with reflected light. A gentle breeze blew as pigeons splashed and bathed in the puddles left from Thursday's melted snow. The leafless trees along Central Park South raised withered fingers to the chalk-colored sky. The doormen standing outside the hotels along the avenue looked sharp in their crisp blue suits, gold buttons sparkling. A chef in white pants and smock stood outside the Plaza Hotel in his chef's hat trying to get a glimpse of the parade as a news crew set up nearby to photograph the event. The smell of horse manure hung in the air from the carriages parked along 59th Street waiting for tourists. It was one of the warmest St. Patrick's Days on record and a great day for the Irish.

Half a million spectators jammed 5th Avenue, squashing Danny and Fidelma against the blue NYC Police Department barricades that separated the sidewalk from the street. The NYPD's Pipe and Drum Corps started a spirited version of "Wild Colonial Boy" as they stepped up the avenue, and the Kerry Pipers of the Bronx, New York, followed close behind.

"Why didn't anyone tell me Brendan was in town?" Danny asked. "What's he doing here, anyway?"

Danny had been back in New York for eight months, after spending a year on a teacher exchange program in Dublin. He'd had the opportunity to extend the program one more year. But after the death of his good friend Father Padraic O'Malley, the parish priest of Ballycara, Danny felt it was time to come home. After his return from Ireland, Danny was hired to teach History and Social Studies at John F. Kennedy High School in the Bronx.

"I just found out this morning," Fidelma answered. "I didn't know he was here either."

Members of the Holy Name Society of the NYC Police Department carried a blue banner. The Ancient Order of Hibernians carried the green, orange, and white flag of Ireland.

"Isn't it ironic that they're being accused of bigotry?" Danny asked as they marched past. The oldest Catholic lay organization in America, the Ancient Order of Hibernians organized the annual parade.

"Who?"

"The AOH. They were formed here in the city in the nineteenth century to fight anti-Irish bigotry. Of course now it's basically a charitable organization for preserving Irish culture and unifying the thirty-two counties of Ireland. But I think it's ironic that the AOH itself is being charged with bigotry for excluding Irish gay organizations from the parade."

"Sure, and why shouldn't they march in the parade?"

"Ask them," Danny said, pointing to the all-male AOH group as it filed past.

Fidelma looped her arm through Danny's as the Cathedral High School All-Girl Marching Band strode by blaring "Wearing of the Green," followed by the Sons of the Ancient Kingdom of Kerry holding a gigantic banner of St. Brendan the Navigator.

"So, the Irish are taking responsibility for the actual founding of America now?" Danny asked, pointing to the banner.

"Every Irish school child knows," Fidelma replied, "that St. Brendan sailed to America in the sixth century. Yes, I'd say that was quite a long time before your man—what's his name?—Columbo?"

Two men held the banner aloft like a sail on poles, while four others—two in front and two in back—controlled the flapping cloth with ropes.

Danny laughed good-naturedly at her tone. "So, where's our own Brendan Grady the Navigator hiding? Why didn't he call me?"

"You know how secretive Brendan is. It makes him feel important," said Fidelma.

Brendan Grady was their mutual friend from Ballycara who, the last time Danny saw him in Ireland, sported a green Mohawk haircut and two silver rings in his left ear. He divided his time between Ballycara and Galway.

"This is a pedestrian crossing," a cop with a bull-horn shouted at a group of onlookers. "You cannot watch the parade from this area."

"My roommate saw Brendan last weekend playing fiddle with a band at a pub near Bainbridge Avenue in the Bronx," said Fidelma.

"Well, I hope he calls."

A gang of carousing young people, swigging green beer from plastic cups, jostled Danny and Fidelma as they shoved through the crowd. Someone else walked by in a green foam-rubber top hat wearing a garish mask with the exaggerated features of a stage Irish-man: thick eyebrows and mustache, bulbous red nose and ears.

Fidelma shuddered. "Don't these people know that St. Patrick's Day is a saint's feast day?"

Hardly anyone, it seemed to Danny, remembered that the parade was meant to honor St. Patrick, who was born to a wealthy family in Roman Britain in the fourth century, captured into slavery at the age of six-teen, and taken to Ireland where he tended sheep for six years.

"It's mostly an excuse to drink beer," said Danny. "Let me tell you, it'll be a rough night for anyone who works in a pub."

St. Patrick escaped, later became a priest, then a bishop. Pope Celestine the First sent him back to Ire-land in four thirty-one, where he converted the Irish to Christianity. This was forgotten in the revelry of St. Patrick's Day in New York. Unless someone men-tioned the snake thing—that Patrick had driven the snakes from Ireland—which was apocryphal, a bunch of blarney.

"Bartenders will make a fortune before the night's over, and every penny of it will be well earned," Danny went on. "Kids from New Jersey and Long Island will wreak havoc in every Irish bar in the city before the night's over—hardly a holy day. Just an excuse to party."

One of the carousers, who had dyed his hair and mustache a fluorescent green, staggered away from his companions, doubled over, and lost his green beer (and his green bowler hat) in the gutter.

"It's a disgrace!"

Danny shrugged. "You're the one who wanted to come."

A drunken young woman in a T-shirt that read GREEN BEER ME ARSE—DRINK TULLAMORE DEW! raised a can of beer in the air and momentarily silenced the din around her with a blood-curdling scream: *"Erin Go Braugh!"*

"I thought St. Patrick had converted the Irish heathens to Christianity," Danny observed.

"Not all of them," said Fidelma. "He didn't get a chance with you American ones."

Just then, the mayor of New York, Marla Silverstein, the first woman to be elected to the office, and Police Commissioner Brian Borkowski, sauntered up the street. They wore Aran sweaters despite the warm temperature and were surrounded by a dozen men in identical navy blue business suits.

"I thought the mayor was supposed to march beside the grand marshal of the parade," said Fidelma.

"Are you kidding?" Danny responded. "Both Mayor Silverstein and the police commissioner have been scrambling to distance themselves as much as possible from Conway.''

Fintan Conway's column had changed over the years from a homey, neighborhood roundup of Irish news, views, and music, to vicious attacks on his enemies, exposés of those who disagreed with him, and rants that swung wildly across the political spectrum. Conway chose controversial topics and he seemed to take whatever side might elicit the most forceful response. In a career spanning four decades, Conway had worked his way up to his current position as the most influential columnist for the *New York Voice.* The sixty-year-old Conway's byline appeared twice a week. In the twenty years of writing his column, he had either befriended or alienated some of the most powerful people in the city.

''The mayor probably agrees with many of his views in private,'' Danny explained, ''but she doesn't want to alienate her constituency by marching up Fifth Avenue with him.''

The NYPD Emerald Society followed carrying green flags, trailed by a band of bagpipers in kilts and tam-o'-shanters. Half a dozen people carried a banner: ENGLAND GET OUT OF IRELAND. Just behind them, the only Japanese entry in the parade, The Tokyo Pipe Band, played ''Amazing Grace'' on the bagpipes.

''Who's minding the store?'' Fidelma asked, obviously referring to the fact that it seemed as if the entire New York City police and fire departments were at the parade.

''I hope somebody is.''

Danny O'Flaherty spotted Fintan Conway's shock of silver hair from almost a block away as his entourage headed up Fifth Avenue. Marching up the avenue with his gray-haired wife beside him, and a couple of tough-looking redheads with the look of rent-a-cops behind, Conway raised a hand to the crowd as if he were a king parading past his subjects.

A helicopter whirred over Central Park and passed above the parade route.

Conway had emigrated from Ireland when he was sixteen years old. Blessed with the Irish flair for language, he had lied about his age, invented a set of phony credentials including a bogus résumé, and landed a job as a copyeditor on the *New York Voice* at the age of seventeen. By the time his hoax was exposed a quarter of a century later, he had already carved out a niche for himself as a shrewd investigative reporter with a brilliant writing style and an instinctual understanding of the man on the street. Far from ruining his career, the discovery of his past made him a celebrity, and he was awarded his own column.

"You know," Fidelma said, "my aunt and uncle knew the Conway family back home."

"That so?"

"Sure, the lot of them were poor as church mice," Fidelma added.

"From Mayo, originally, weren't they?" asked Danny.

The Rose of Tralee, her raven hair flying in the breeze, walked bravely up the avenue, tottering in her uncomfortable-looking high-heeled shoes as she waved to the St. Patrick's Day crowd swelling the sidewalks.

"That's right. The family owned a worthless farm on the side of Croagh Patrick."

"The holy mountain?"

"Yeah. But their land sloped so much they couldn't even grow potatoes."

Forget potatoes. Conway planted his roots in New York and cultivated political connections among Irish-Americans, especially in labor unions—in particular the Brotherhood of Electrical Workers Union and the Plumbers Union. He wielded power in the Irish-American communities of Upper Manhattan and the Bronx like an old-time ward boss. He found people jobs, helped newcomers get green cards, sent flowers on birthdays, loaned people money, attended weddings, wakes, and funerals. But there was a price for these services. Separation of editorial from ad sales and separation of political favors from endorsements in his columns were concepts completely unknown to Fintan Patrick Conway. He showed no loyalty to any political ideology: far right on some issues, far left on others, but rarely in the center.

Conway marched forward in his gray suit swinging a two-foot-long *shillelagh* and sporting a white tie printed with green shamrocks. He held out his hand to the crowd pressed against the barriers on the opposite side of the street. As Conway reached into the pack and shook hands with four or five people, Danny saw the guy in the goofy hat and mask—what was he supposed to be, a leprechaun?—reach out toward the grand marshal. Something glimmered in the leprechaun's hand, like a flashbulb.

Danny turned away in disgust. He hated the St. Patrick's Day parade and wished he had not let Fidelma talk him into coming. It saddened Danny that Irish culture had been so trivialized. A proud culture of poets and scholars that had seen millions of its people starve to death and continued even today to fight political oppression had been reduced in the popular imagination to leprechauns and shamrocks, drunks and priests. This guy in the mask's idea of celebrating his heritage was to dress up in the most degrading caricature of an Irishman and walk around taking photos and looking like an idiot. Were the Irish the only ethnic group that did that to themselves? Did British colonialism breed this kind of self-loathing? Could you imagine an Italian at the San Gennaro festival dressed—

Suddenly Danny heard a high-pitched scream and he looked back to see Conway staggering slightly as if he'd stumbled on a loose stone. The grand marshal spun away from his wife, clutching his heart.

"What's wrong with him?" Fidelma asked.

Conway dropped to one knee and held that position for a moment as he rocked back and forth. His bright red face had turned white as he opened his mouth trying to get a gulp of air.

"My Lord," said Fidelma, "I think he's having a heart attack."

For a moment the noise of the parade ceased. Then Danny heard more shrieks as Conway rocked back and forth on one knee. His wife held him by the arm to keep him from falling as she cried for help. Then he lowered himself slowly and fell on both knees as if praying. His eyes were wide as half-dollars, and he had an excruciating look of horror on his face.

"What in God's name?" Fidelma gasped.

Conway held the praying position for at least half a minute.

"He's having a stroke!"

Then the grand marshal pitched forward face-down in the street.

People swirled around Danny and Fidelma, shouting and pushing. Members of the County Cork Pipes and Drums Band marching behind Conway crashed into one another as the parade ground to a halt, and hundreds of cops swarmed over the site. People started to run, and Danny watched as a boy fell in the street and was kicked in the chin. He tried to reach the crying boy who shouted, "Mommy!" but the stampeding crowd overwhelmed him.

Conway's wife sat down on the curb and pulled her husband into her arms. He lay slumped in her lap as she cradled him. Danny saw blood on the silk white, orange, and green grand marshal sash.

Just as someone screamed "Get an ambulance," Danny heard the shriek of sirens coming from three different directions. A fight broke out between two drunken revelers as people shoved, pushed, and stepped on one another to make way for the ambulance that inched its way through the crowd.

"Don't push!"

"Get out of the way!"

"I said don't push me!"

Two police officers ripped aside a wooden police barrier and let the ambulance through.

The doors of the red and white Fire Department ambulance flew open and three paramedics in white pants and blue FDNY sweatshirts fought through the crowd to where Conway lay gasping in his wife's lap. By now, a chain of blue-suited NYPD officers surrounded the fallen grand marshal and shoved people back to let the EMTs through. "Get back. I said, get back!"

The group of young revelers standing beside Danny pointed to the roof of the nineteen-story Plaza Hotel across the street.

"Get back!" the cops continued to shout.

"What are they pointing at?" Fidelma asked.

Danny looked up to the hotel where some of the windows were open to catch the unexpected nice weather.

Mrs. Conway stroked her husband's silver hair and a spot of blood stained her white lace dress. The EMTs wrenched him free of his wife's hysterical grasp, checked his breathing and pulse, pulled off his tie and cut open his shirt with a pair of surgical shears, then covered his mouth with an oxygen mask and eased him onto an aluminum scoop.

"Did he have a stroke, do you think?" Fidelma whispered as she and Danny stepped away from the barriers to clear the way.

"I don't know. He's bleeding."

"I think he smacked his head when he fell," said Fidelma.

"Clear the area!" A policeman with a bullhorn shouted. "Go home. We're closing this section of Fifth Avenue. I said clear the area!"

As the siren shrieked on the ambulance carrying Conway, swarms of people raced about knocking into one another, not sure what to do or where to go.

"Clear the area!"

Almost immediately, a camera crew ran down Fifth Avenue lugging equipment.

Dominick Carter of *New York 1 News* shouted into a microphone while the cameras rolled. "...total pandemonium here at the St. Patrick's Day parade on Fifth Avenue. Grand marshal of the parade, Fintan

Conway, has collapsed. It's not clear at this point what's wrong."

"*GET BACK!*"

"Conway appears to be alive but he's just been taken from the area in an ambulance. I'm afraid this is going to be a sad St. Patrick's Day for a lot of people. And it looks like the luck of the Irish may have run out," the newsman summed up, "for the controversial grand marshal, Fintan Conway."

THREE

UNIFORMED POLICE OFFICERS roped off a thirty-square-foot area with yellow plastic tape where Conway had fallen. Several patrol units arrived with more uniformed officers. One of them, a Latina, yelled into her radio: "Get the Major Crime Scene Unit down here now."

"What are they doing?" asked Fidelma.

"I don't know."

Danny and Fidelma watched as the cops canvassed the area asking people what they had seen. Within five minutes, two plainclothes NYPD detectives arrived in an unmarked car.

"Hey, you!" the older of the two shouted at one of the uniformed officers. "You're tracking blood all over the place. Make yourself useful—get all these people out of the way. I want this entire block sealed off, not just this area. Move those barricades over here and get all these people out of the way now! And you," he yelled at another officer, "start taking statements."

"This is not about a stroke or a heart attack," Danny said.

Sirens screeched, throwing globes of red light across the detectives' backs as they ducked under the yellow crime scene tape and stood beside a small puddle of blood where Conway had fallen.

The older of the two NYPD detectives knelt on one knee beside the puddle. A black man, he wore a well-pressed navy blue suit, crisp white shirt, and a sky-blue silk tie. His fine, sharp features looked as if they'd been chiseled from obsidian. He furrowed the gray brows above his bloodshot eyes that darted around the scene, and clenched his jaws. His gray hair and mustache brought his features together in a way that suggested to Danny detached resignation to the horrors to which his job exposed him.

The detective took a handkerchief from the top pocket of his jacket and picked up Conway's *shillelagh,* looked at it, shrugged, and handed it to the other detective—a blue-eyed sandy-haired man in his early thirties—who took it to their car.

When the detective stood up, Danny saw him raise his hands as if to make an announcement. "Did anyone see anything?" he yelled in a booming voice.

"Let's get out of here, Danny," Fidelma said nervously.

"Hold on a second."

Fidelma shared a studio across from Van Cortland Park in the Bronx with another Irish woman recently arrived in the States. Fidelma was technically an illegal immigrant. Danny had contacted an immigration lawyer and was doing everything he could to help her get resident status. But he knew she was worried the police might ask for her identification.

"Did anybody see anything at all?" the detective yelled again.

"Come on, Danny. Let's go."

"Wait a minute." Danny motioned to the officer. "I think…"

"Don't get involved," Fidelma whispered. "You didn't see anything, did you?"

Danny stepped forward and motioned again to the detective. "I think I did see something."

The black policeman moved straight toward Danny. He flipped his jacket away, revealing his detective shield on his belt next to a holstered .9mm Glock. He extended a hand to Danny and Fidelma and they both shook it.

"I'm Detective George Washington." He held up the palms of his hands. "Save the wisecracks. What did you see?"

Fidelma started speaking in a rush of words.

"Hold on. You stand over there by my partner," Washington said to Fidelma, "while I talk to your friend here."

As Fidelma stepped away toward the sandy-haired detective, Danny saw a troop of uniformed patrolmen moving toward the Plaza. Two cops with rifles stood on the roof of the French Renaissance-style hotel, surveying the scene below.

The detective glanced around the area, now swarming with cops, then looked at Danny. "You saw something?"

"I don't know. There was this guy in a mask."

"How do you know it was a guy if he wore a mask?"

"Oh." Danny stopped and tried to recreate the scene in his head just before the grand marshal seemed to trip. "Well. You're right, I guess. Okay, there was this person in a great big…like foam-rubber top hat."

Detective Washington looked at Danny skeptically. But he asked calmly, "What color was the hat?"

"Green."

"Go on."

"And he wore this mask. Like a caricature mask of an Irishman or a leprechaun or something. I saw him about forty-five minutes ago with a bunch of kids who were drinking beer."

Washington sighed.

"But then I saw him again," Danny said, trying to remember. He pointed across the street. "He was over there. Right where Conway fell. As the grand marshal passed I saw him reach out like he was trying to touch him. I thought he was taking a picture."

"Okay."

"Then I looked somewhere else. I didn't see him again."

"So you saw a leprechaun in a green hat taking pictures. What does that have to do—"

"When I looked back, that's when Conway stumbled, and then he fell down. What happened to him, anyway?" Danny asked as if suddenly remembering what it was all about.

"That's what we're trying to find out."

"Did he get shot?"

"Did you *hear* any shots?" Washington asked.

"No," Danny said. "No. I heard someone scream. Then I saw Conway kneel down. No, I didn't hear any shots."

"Are you sure?"

"Yeah."

"Did this guy in the mask have a gun?"

"No. I mean, I didn't see a gun. But something

flashed in his hand. I assumed it was a camera with a flash.''

"Why use a flash in the daytime?'' asked Washington.

"I don't know.''

"You're sure you didn't see a gun?''

"I don't think so. Maybe... No.''

"Which one?''

"What?'' Danny asked.

"You don't think so? Maybe? Or no?''

"No,'' Danny said confidently.

"Then why mention this guy in the mask at all? Why ask if Conway got shot?''

"I don't know. It was weird. The way this person in the mask reached out like that. Like he was trying to touch the grand marshal. Then the flash.''

"You're sure you didn't hear any shots?''

Danny nodded toward the hotel. "I saw people pointing up to the Plaza. Maybe they heard—''

"I'm asking you. That's why we separate witnesses, so they don't start telling each other's stories.''

Danny hesitated a beat. "I don't really think I heard anything other than what I've told you.''

"Good answer. I wish more people were that honest. What time did you see this...person with the mask?''

Danny glanced at his watch. "The first time about forty-five minutes ago. Then, when he reached out, that was about twenty minutes ago. I'd say about twelve-fifty.''

"How tall?''

"Maybe six-one, six-two.''

"What happened to him?''

"Or her?" Danny asked.

Washington winced as if he'd been reprimanded. "Yes. Yes."

"I didn't see the person in the hat and mask again. Actually I didn't think about it until after you came. I thought it was just some idiot dressed up in an insulting costume for St. Patrick's Day."

"Probably that's all it was," Washington said. "What else did you see? Anyone running from the scene? Anyone acting oddly?"

Danny thought for a moment. "Not really."

"You got some identification?"

Danny fished his New York State driver's license from his wallet and handed it over. "Did Conway get shot?" he asked. "Is that why he was bleeding?"

Washington looked at the license and handed it back. "Mr. O'Flaherty, I'm here to try to find out what did happen. Let's try it again. You see anyone who seemed out of place?"

"There were hundreds of people here."

"Somebody who seemed like he didn't belong at the parade?"

Danny couldn't imagine anyone who could possibly look out of place at the St. Patrick's Day parade. It was the one day in New York when everyone claimed to be Irish. "I really can't say for sure."

By now the vicinity in and around the yellow crime scene tape was crowded with uniformed police officers, a woman from the Photo Unit taking snapshots of the area, technicians from the Mobile Crime Unit, and dozens of other official-looking men and women.

"Now, can you tell me anything else you remember?"

"Not really."

Danny glanced at Fidelma talking nervously with Washington's partner. Then the partner sauntered over and whispered something to the detective.

When his partner left, Washington looked at Danny. "Your girlfriend's got a heavy accent."

"She's Irish, but listen—"

"Oh, really?" Washington said in mock surprise. "I thought it was South Carolina."

"Listen, she—"

"No, you listen to me." Detective Washington just looked at Danny, waiting.

"Yes, sir."

"Tell her to stop worrying. We're not going to call the INS. We've got better things to do than to round up illegal Harps."

A uniformed officer came up and handed Washington a paper cup of steaming coffee. "Here you are, sir."

"Thanks. Listen, this guy's girlfriend can go home," he said to the officer. Detective Washington dug in the breast pocket of his jacket, came up with a business card, and handed it to Danny. "If you do remember anything else give me a call."

Danny took the card, glanced at it, and put it in his wallet. "I'll let you know if I think of anything."

"You do that. In the meantime, you're going down to the precinct." He turned to the officer. "I want you to take a full statement from Mr. O'Flaherty here about what he saw. Either he's had too much to drink and was seeing leprechauns or he's the only witness we've got so far."

FOUR

DANNY'S PHONE RANG at 6:30 the next morning, Sunday, March 18th, waking him from a dream. He had spent a couple of hours at the 19th Precinct the day before giving a full, signed statement concerning everything he had witnessed at the parade. Then he went home and slept like the dead. In the dream, Danny owned the O'Flaherty funeral parlor downstairs and his father was his employee. Even though Danny knew his father was dead, they were embalming the body of a little girl and his father was giving advice. *Look,* Danny said in the dream. *I'm the boss here now. I'm the boss here. I'm the boss...* The phone rang again.

"Hello? *Hello?*"

Danny slammed the phone down and lay there staring at the ceiling, unable to get back to sleep.

Danny O'Flaherty lived on 207th Street in Upper Manhattan above the O'Flaherty Funeral Parlor. Danny's father, a mortician, or funeral director as he preferred to be called, had run the establishment until his death from a heart attack in 1995. Now Danny lived alone in the two-bedroom apartment in the prewar building, furnished with antiques left by his parents, as well as a couple pieces he had picked up himself—a Queen Anne camel-back sofa and a Duncan Phyfe dining room table and chairs. He had cleared the walls of the crucifixes and religious art that his parents had hoarded and replaced them with framed prints of a more secular nature, including dozens of maps. A globe that he sometimes used in his classroom sat in a corner of the living room on a wooden stand. He had turned one of the bedrooms into an office where he had a computer and printer as well as hundreds of books and texts. A huge map of Ireland took up a large portion of the office wall.

Danny had two older sisters. Anne lived in Riverdale and worked as an administrative assistant for the NYPD in the 34th Precinct. Mary was the principal of a Catholic school in Yonkers. His four younger brothers—Patrick, Joseph, David, and Michael—were spread throughout the country.

After lying there for a few minutes, Danny threw off the sheet and swung his legs out of bed. Might as well go get the paper as long as I'm up, he thought. He slipped into a pair of jeans, an Aran sweater he'd picked up in Donegal, and tennis shoes. He went into the bathroom and ran a comb through his hair. Looking briefly at his reflection in the mirror above the sink, Danny noted a few more gray hairs among the silver threads already woven into the shag of black curls on his head. His bushy eyebrows grew together above his soft brown eyes and a reddish mustache set off his not-infrequent smile. But the murder of his friend Father O'Malley last year in Ireland had taken the twinkle from his eyes.

Danny walked down the stairs from his apartment. A raw wind slapped him as he crossed the street to the bodega. The sky was dark and overcast. The good weather of St. Patrick's Day had vanished as suddenly as it appeared, and the chilly air was laden with moisture.

Danny had lived in this neighborhood for most of his life and was oblivious to the honking horns, car alarms, shrieking sirens, and shouts of children that echoed in the street. The thump of *merengue* and hip-hop music reverberated from oversized speakers in the open trunks of parked cars.

The few Irish left in Danny's formerly near all-Irish neighborhood were often elderly, or younger Irish-Americans, sometimes derisively called Narrowbacks, who had inherited their immigrant parents' rent-controlled apartments. The Irish pubs still left in Inwood, from the Irish Brigade, Irish Eyes, Patrick's, The Piper's Kilt, to The Liffey Pub, were like shrines to a dying cult that gathered there to remember the past. The future was written in Spanish and the old drunks hunched over boilermakers wanted no part of it even if they shared pews with the newcomers at Our Lady Queen of Martyrs and Good Shepherd Catholic Churches.

Danny entered the tiny bodega across from his apartment and bought a copy of the Sunday *New York Daily News*.

LUCK RUNS OUT FOR CONWAY

The Daily News, with its flair for tacky headlines, had picked up the "luck of the Irish" cliché and managed to combine tastelessness with a tantalizing lead that drew Danny into the story.

Fintan Conway, grand marshal of this year's St. Patrick's Day parade, was shot down yesterday

on Fifth Avenue. Paramedics rushed him to St.
Luke's Roosevelt Hospital where he is in critical
condition with bullet wounds to the chest and
right arm.

So he *had* been shot. If it was the guy in the mask
who shot him, he must have used a silencer.

Danny skimmed the article. Conway was still alive,
barely surviving on life support. His wife was quoted
saying that if Fintan died, she hoped whoever was
responsible would get the hot shot.

Lethal injection? Danny remembered that fierce opposition to the death penalty was another one of Conway's stands. What a thing for his wife to say.
Though Conway had expressed anti-gay views that
had earned him legions of enemies, his equally ve-
hement anti-death penalty stands had endeared him to
some liberals and alienated conservative readers.
When the pope had visited the U.S., asking leaders to
do away with capital punishment and abortion, Conway wrote that the pope should mind his own business on abortion but he supported the pope's stance
against the death penalty.

But why would Conway's wife mention capital
punishment for the perpetrator? Conway wasn't even
dead.

Danny bought a *café con leche* to go, and read the
story as he crossed back to his apartment. Police had
moved quickly, arresting an illegal immigrant from
Ireland who had been discovered near the scene with
physical evidence linking him to the crime. It was
believed that he either shot the grand marshal with a
high-powered rifle from a room in the Plaza Hotel or
a co-conspirator had shot him from the street using a

silenced handgun. That's why they hadn't heard any shots, thought Danny. The nature of the evidence, said Police Commissioner Brian Borkowski, was not being disclosed at this time pending further investigation.

Although Danny had spent two hours at the 19th Precinct going over the story about the person in the hat and mask, the more he talked about it with detectives, the less sure Danny was that it had anything to do with Conway. Now he realized it really could have been the person in the mask who had shot him after all.

The phone rang as Danny let himself into his apartment. He moved his cat, Barnabas, from his favorite chair, sat down, and picked up the phone.

"Hello?"

"Have you seen the papers?" asked Fidelma.

"Yes. I just bought one. I'm reading about the parade right now." He rubbed his eyes and looked down at the paper.

"Conway did get shot," Fidelma said. "And you saw who did it."

"No. I didn't see—"

"But you told the police you—"

Danny's eyes jumped back to the middle of the article—how could he have missed it? His heart pounded as he quickly reread the passage, then looked up. He felt disoriented, dizzy, out of breath.

"Danny?"

"What the..." His eyes darted back to the paper again. The illegal Irish immigrant charged with the attempted murder of Fintan Conway was Danny's old friend, Brendan Grady. "My God, I can't believe this. They've arrested Brendan."

"Ah, and that has to be wrong. Rubbish," Fidelma said vehemently. "Brendan Grady wouldn't hurt a soul. You Americans with your guns all over the place!"

"Look, Fidelma, my cousin Rose was murdered in your own quaint little village."

"Well, no one *shot* her."

"Oh, no, just bludgeoned her to death with a shovel. And what about Father O'Malley? Besides, there's evidence linking Brendan to the crime."

"What evidence?"

"The paper doesn't say."

"Exactly!"

Danny stood up and paced the living room, his portable phone clapped to his ear. Brendan Grady, like Fidelma, was also from the village of Ballycara in County Clare where Danny's grandfather had been born. Danny knew Brendan well from his visits to Ireland.

"There's got to be some mistake," Danny whispered.

"This is just not possible," Fidelma added. "I've known Brendan since we were children."

"But you have to admit," Danny said, "Brendan's always been a bit elusive."

"What in the world do you mean?"

"You said yourself he was secretive."

"Ah, that just makes him feel important," Fidelma responded.

"Still, no one in Ballycara seems to know why he spends so much time in Galway." Danny sat down.

"That's cod," said Fidelma. "Sure, he likes the bright lights. Ballycara's not exactly Manhattan."

"Neither is Galway! What was he doing in New York, anyway?"

"He's with a band, sure. I told you they've been playing a pub up in the Bronx."

"Where?"

"O'Dwyer's."

Danny's cat jumped up and curled into a ball on his lap. Barnabas always knew when Danny was upset. Danny stroked the fur along his back, reached over and snapped the TV on with a remote, and scrolled to New York's all-news channel, *New York One*.

"...grand marshal of the St. Patrick's Day Parade was shot down on Fifth Avenue yesterday. Informed sources are saying that an illegal Irish immigrant is believed to have shot Conway with a high-powered weapon from the ninth floor of the Plaza Hotel."

"Now they're saying he was shot from the Plaza again," said Danny.

"Someone's got to help Brendan," said Fidelma.

"What do you mean?"

"He's illegal. He's all by himself."

"How is he illegal?" Danny asked.

"I told you he's been playing in a band in the Bronx. He's working without a permit."

"I see."

"You said you saw someone reach out toward Conway," began Fidelma. "The fellow in the mask. Something flashed in his hand. He probably had a gun—"

"Now wait a minute, Fidelma."

"You've got to help him."

"What are you talking about? You're the one who told me not to get involved."

"That was before this."

"Oh, now everything's different. Brendan doesn't need my help. He needs a lawyer."

"Sure, and how will he afford a lawyer?"

Danny said nothing as he gently stroked Barnabas.

"Well?" Fidelma demanded.

"Well what? In this country a lawyer is appointed to you by the court if you can't afford one."

"Can't *you* do something?"

"What can I do? The New York City Police Department will take care of this. That's what we pay taxes for."

Fidelma was silent at the other end of the line.

"I gave a complete statement at the Nineteenth Precinct," said Danny. "Believe me, this Detective Washington is in complete control."

There was another long pause.

"I'm a high school teacher, for goodness sake! Fidelma, we've got to see how this all plays out. If he's done nothing he'll be cleared."

"You said you saw something."

"Fidelma, everything happened so fast. We didn't even realize he'd been shot yesterday. You thought he was having a stroke. I don't know why I even mentioned that idiot in the mask. If Brendan's done nothing, he'll be cleared."

"You're so sure of that, are you?"

"Yes, I am," Danny said, but he wondered what *would* happen to Brendan. In fact, how could he be sure Brendan wasn't involved? After all, it was well known in Ireland that he had IRA connections. And hadn't Fintan Conway attacked the IRA in one of his columns?

"I want to go see him, Danny. He needs help."

"What about Conway? He *really* needs help."

Fidelma sighed, that note of exasperation creeping into her voice that made Danny feel as though he was getting into something over his head.

Even Barnabas squirmed in Danny's lap.

"Will you go with me to see Brendan?" she asked.

"We don't even know where he is."

"I do."

"Where?"

"A place called Rikers Island."

FIVE

"MR. O'FLAHERTY?" Joey Rodriguez sat in the back of the classroom waving his hand to get Danny's attention. "Mr. O'Flaherty?"

Danny pulled back his shirt sleeve and checked his watch. Five minutes to go in the last period on Monday, March 19th. Danny had been trying to get the class ready for a test on Wednesday covering the Irish Famine.

"What is it, Joey?"

Joey Rodriguez had been a student of Danny's for almost three years. He had first taught Joey at Our Lady Queen of Martyrs Elementary School. The boy was born in the neighborhood—on 204th Street—to an Irish-American mother and a Dominican father. Joey was in Danny's sixth grade class the year Joey's father was killed in the crossfire of a drug war being waged in Washington Heights. Whether the father was himself involved in the crack trade was never really known—at least not to Danny. When he returned after missing two weeks of summer school for his father's funeral—the body was buried in Santo Domingo—Joey's behavior had already begun to deteriorate. Now he was a senior in Danny's last period Social Studies class.

"Yes, Joey?"

"Yo, Teach. Like why we got to study all this Irish Famine crap? Who cares about a bunch of rotten potatoes? That junk's old and cold, man."

Danny liked Joey. He was a smart boy who had grown up too fast in the sometimes dangerous atmosphere of Upper Manhattan. The boy needed a stronger hand at home, but his mother juggled a receptionist job by day and a waitress job at night in order to maintain Joey and his two younger sisters. This was not uncommon among Danny's students, which was one reason the school system expected teachers not only to teach their subjects, but to teach values, manners, responsibility, social skills, conflict management, you name it. Every time a social crisis emerged, Danny thought, the schools threw the responsibility for fixing it on teachers. How could parents be expected to raise their own children? They had to go to work.

Danny had known Joey's mother, Kate McNamara, in high school long before she married Joey's father, Tito Rodriguez. Danny and Kate had been friends. More than friends. But that was a long time ago.

Danny made a special effort to get through to Joey Rodriguez. Joey was his project for the year. It probably would take a miracle to get through to him.

Danny looked at Joey thoughtfully. "You don't have to study anything, Joey."

"Say what?"

"You're welcome to grow up without any knowledge of your past."

"It ain't my past!"

"It's at least half of your past."

"I'm Dominican," said Joey.

"Good. You should be proud of that. But we already had a section on the Dominican Republic. You blew that test.''

Unlike his other classmates, who were well-adjusted kids for the most part, by the time Joey had graduated from the Catholic elementary school where Danny taught for years, he had moved on to glue-sniffing and hanging out on the corner of 207th Street and Nagle Avenue under the elevated subway tracks with a group of tough neighborhood kids. Danny had seen them smoking pot and passing a bottle of white rum on numerous afternoons after school. Some of the boys wore the colors of the Latin Kings. Danny hoped Joey was not getting pulled into that gang.

''The past belongs to everyone, Joey. History is a story. But it's *owned* by those who tell the story.''

''Huh?''

Just then the bell rang and the students gathered their books and papers.

Danny was as anxious to get out of class as the students were. After he'd finished talking to Fidelma last night, he had called Don Boyle, the chairman of the NYC St. Patrick's Day Parade and Celebration Committee, and arranged to meet with him today at 5:00 p.m. Boyle remembered Danny's father and said he'd tell him everything he could about the parade. Then Danny had called Fidelma back. ''I'm not promising anything,'' he had told her. ''But I'll meet with the chairman of the parade committee and see what I can find out about Conway.''

''Review chapters nine through thirteen,'' Danny shouted above the din of the classroom. ''And pay special attention to the causes of the Famine. You can be sure there'll be an essay question on that.''

The few students listening groaned as they left the

class. Danny gathered his books and notes and stowed them in his briefcase.

"Joey," Danny said, calling the boy back to his desk before he left.

"What?"

"I'd like a word with you."

Joey swaggered up to the desk with a grin on his face. "Yo, Teach. What it is?" He wore baggy blue jeans slung around the base of his hips with a belt several sizes too large looped around the pants. The tops of his boxer shorts stuck out above the belt. His baseball cap was turned backward on his head and the laces of his sneakers were untied.

Kids who dressed like that in my school days, Danny thought, couldn't afford anything better. Now this was the style, and the clothes cost a fortune. "Is something bothering you, Joey?"

"What you talking 'bout? Nothing bothering me."

"Are you ready for the test on Wednesday?"

"Piece of cake."

"How's your mother?"

Joey's grin disappeared and he lowered his head. He squeaked the toe of his Reebok sneaker on the floor and fumbled with the zipper on his Tommy Hilfiger jacket.

"Is she still working two jobs?"

"Yeah."

"Are you helping out around the house?"

Joey, still staring at the floor, mumbled something.

"Joey," Danny began, trying his best not to sound too adult and uncool although he suspected it was probably hopeless, "those boys under the elevated tracks are going to get you in trouble."

Joey's cold blue eyes snapped up. "Don't disrespect my homies."

"Your *homeboys* might get you killed."

Joey shrugged into his jacket and turned to leave.

"Study for the test, Joey." Danny picked up his briefcase. "And don't forget the causes of the Famine."

"I don't care nothing 'bout all that bull—"

"Watch it, Joey," Danny said. "You might not care about it, but you need to do well on that test. Blow it and you could fail this class."

"So what?"

"You want to graduate, don't you?"

Joey said nothing.

"Study for the test," Danny said again.

Sometimes Danny wondered how much longer he could put up with teaching in the city. His brothers and sisters often asked him why he stayed. Teachers in the suburbs—in Westchester and Suffolk Counties—made at least twenty-five percent more than city teachers and had to deal with fewer problems.

Often, Danny thought of going back to Ireland and working for the teacher-exchange program again. Ireland had changed dramatically in the two decades since Danny had first gone there with his mother. Back then, Ireland still retained many of the traditional aspects of its culture. Now, the country belonged to the European Union and enjoyed strong economic growth. The Celtic Tiger—the strong Irish economy—was all the talk.

There were fewer and fewer of the traditional thatch-roofed cottages and more of the slate and pebbledash ranch-style homes. More unbelievably, job fairs were being held in New York to recruit workers for the booming Irish economy. This reversed a centuries-old pattern of Irish men and women going abroad to find work. Danny found it ironic that all four of his grandparents had fled Ireland for economic reasons. Now, he seriously considered going back.

But Danny stayed in New York. He found, unlike countless others, that he could handle the public school system. During his first couple of years he was still trying to save the world. Now, he just tried to do the best job he could. With all the pressure and extra work the school system put on teachers, Danny sometimes resented the administration. Many of the head office types were so far removed from the daily work of a schoolteacher, they may as well have been on another planet. Still, Danny liked his job. Early in his career, when he worried about whether he was really teaching the kids anything, Danny set a simple goal for himself: All he needed to do was make the class function. But on top of that, he'd do his best to turn one kid around completely. If he could perform a minor miracle on just one kid, or if he saved one student from a life of street crime and drugs, he could consider himself a successful teacher.

WHEN DANNY walked out the front entrance of the school, he noticed a green Mercedes Benz with two men in front parked across the street. At first he didn't think anything about it. But as Danny stood alone waiting for the bus, he had the feeling the men were watching him. They certainly weren't there to pick up kids from school. The driver smoked a cigarette and stared straight ahead. Danny thought he saw the driver glance back at the bus stop in the side-mirror.

When the bus finally arrived, Danny fished his Metrocard from his top pocket and climbed aboard. He made his way to the back and found a seat by the rear door. He dropped his briefcase on the empty seat next to him. As the bus pulled away from the curb, Danny looked through the rear window and saw the Mercedes make a U-turn and swing into traffic behind the bus. Strange.

Danny opened his briefcase, took a stack of essays from his morning classes, and started correcting them. He was a tough but fair grader and he worked carefully through the essays. Five minutes later he glanced behind him again and saw the green Mercedes following closely.

The car continued to follow Danny's bus across the Bronx and over the University Heights Bridge. When Danny got out at the corner of Broadway and 207th Street, the Mercedes slid into a parking space across the street from his apartment.

Nobody got out of the car.

Upstairs, Danny made a ham and Swiss on rye, and reheated a cup of that morning's coffee in the microwave. The dishes from this morning were still piled in the sink. No matter how homey Danny had made the apartment, it still looked like a bachelor's pad. Danny hoped that someday Fidelma would share the apartment with him, but he had still not worked up the nerve to pop the question. He wasn't quite sure he was ready for marriage. But if he didn't do something soon he was afraid he might end up a bachelor for life. He had considered asking Fidelma to just move in with him. Although the Church's grip on Fidelma had loosened somewhat since she had moved to New York from Ireland, "living in sin" was not something she took lightly. Danny loved her. He had hinted broadly to Fidelma that maybe it was time he found someone to share his life—and his apartment—with him. He knew that the only way was to marry her. But he was just not sure he was ready. And he had never actually used the "M" word with her.

As he sipped his coffee, he pushed aside the curtain of his kitchen window overlooking the street and saw the green Mercedes with two men sitting in it still parked across the street in front of the deli. Were they really watching for him? Was it just a coincidence that brought them to Danny's street?

When he finished his sandwich, Danny fed Barnabas, changed his water and litter box, and went to the basement of the building. He walked through the laundry, across the super's workroom, and exited the building through a side door into the alley. If those men in the Mercedes were watching his apartment for some reason, Danny wanted to make sure they didn't follow him...not that he thought he was *really* being followed, though.

He went to the back of the alley, climbed over a chain-link fence leading to another alley and emerged on 208th Street. He looked to make sure the green Mercedes was nowhere in sight, then walked back to the subway station and caught a downtown A-Train to 168th Street.

At 168th Street, Danny turned uptown, walked past Bab's Discount Clothing, Mike's Bagel, and Famiglia Pizzeria. He glanced behind to make sure no one was following him. He didn't think anyone was, but why would anyone be following *him*, anyway?

Danny pushed past a group of nurses from Columbia Presbyterian in starched white pants and smocks, and interns with stethoscopes around their necks, and walked into Coogan's Restaurant and Pub on Broadway and 168th Street a few minutes past five.

SIX

DANNY FOUND DON BOYLE sitting in a booth in the back of the lounge. The booth looked toward the mahogany bar crowded with interns and nurses ending their shifts at Columbia Presbyterian Medical Center, Dominicans from the neighborhood, and a smattering of red-faced Irish regulars who still lived nearby. Green-shaded lamps hung on chains from the ceiling and the kelly-green walls were covered with framed photos of Irish boxers, clippings from the *Irish Echo*, and the *Irish Voice*, columns from the *Daily News* by Jim Dwyer and from the *New York Voice* by Fintan Conway. A certificate of appreciation from the Detectives Endowment Association of the New York City Police Department hung on a wall behind the bar. The 34th Precinct House was on Broadway and 183rd Street and Coogan's had long been a favorite hangout for cops from the station house.

"Finn Conway is an idiot," Don Boyle said when Danny asked his opinion of the grand marshal.

Danny was well aware, from reading the *Irish Echo*, of the complexity of the St. Patrick's Day parade committee and the bitterness of the ongoing feuds between the committee and members of the various Emerald Societies. When a previous committee had considered former Irish Republican prisoner Joe

Doherty as a possible candidate for grand marshal it had caused bitter dissension among the committee ranks. Joe Doherty had escaped from jail in Belfast following a shootout in 1980 with his unit of the IRA that left a British officer dead, and had fled to the U.S. He was captured by the FBI in New York in 1983 as he tended bar at Clancy's on 3rd Avenue.

"I was the first to tell the parade committee that Joe Doherty was precisely the kind of grand marshal that the parade should *not* have," said Don Boyle. "Most of them just don't seem to get it. The grand marshal is a figurehead. It's all about PR. Take Maureen O'Hara, the last grand marshal of the twentieth century and everything a grand marshal should be. Well, Fintan Conway was an even worse choice than Joe Doherty would have been. A public relations disaster."

Don Boyle did not mention the more recent controversy surrounding the parade, but Danny knew all about it. An ad-hoc investigation committee composed of representatives of various Emerald Societies had formed to look into misuse of funds by the parade organizers. Known as the Save the St. Patrick's Day Committee, it had enlisted the support of the attorney general of New York to investigate public officials and labor unions involved in the parade.

"Can I get you gentlemen something?" the waitress asked as she approached their booth.

"Pint of Harp," said Danny.

Don Boyle held up a half-empty drink. "Bring me another Dewar's and water."

The committee also examined the use of parade funds over the last ten or eleven years because they believed there had been some double-dealing and under-the-table shenanigans going on. It didn't surprise Danny that Don Boyle side-stepped discussion of this more recent investigation, since Boyle would have been one of those who had been investigated.

But most of all, Danny knew, the investigating committee wanted some accounting from the parade committee as to how money was spent, and who had final say in the selection of the grand marshal. Boyle didn't bring that up, either.

All this over a parade.

Who else but the Irish, Danny thought, could turn something that was supposed to be fun into so much conflict that half the marchers had teeth marks on their shirts from all the backbiting?

"One question on the minds of a lot of people," Boyle volunteered, "is why the Ford Motor Company leads the parade every year despite having a reputation for job discrimination against Catholics in Northern Ireland. I asked Finn Conway to address that in one of his columns. You think he did? No way! Wouldn't touch it."

"Why not?"

"Who knows? He's probably been bought out."

The waitress came back and set their drinks in front of them.

"Let me give you some background on the parade," Boyle began as he took a sip of his fresh drink. "The first St. Paddy's Day parade in New York was held downtown on March seventeenth, seventeen seventy-six, with Irishmen in a military unit that policed the American colonies before the Revolution."

Danny stifled a yawn and reached for his pint. As parade committee chairman, Boyle was a storehouse of information on everything concerning the parade.

But Danny had the feeling he was trying to avoid talking about Fintan Conway.

"Every year since then there's been a parade. It wasn't until the eighteen-twenties that the individual Irish societies began their own parades, marching to St. Patrick's Cathedral or one of the other Catholic churches. After eighteen fifty-one, the individual parades were consolidated under a single grand marshal." Boyle stopped his monologue and looked at Danny with a bitter expression. "Fintan Conway was the worst choice for grand marshal ever made in the history of the parade."

Danny cleared his throat. "Why do you say that?"

The bouncer, a six-foot-five black man, with one arm the size of a side of beef and the other a stump where it had been amputated at the shoulder, circulated through the crowd of after-office drinkers wearing a white ten-gallon cowboy hat and a threatening smile. He stood briefly beside Danny's table, then moved on.

Boyle reached into the pocket of his suit jacket lying beside him and took out a package of imported cigarettes—Woodbines. "Smoke?" he asked, offering Danny the pack.

"No thanks." Danny examined Boyle. The chairman had a red face, and a purple spiderweb of broken blood vessels mottled his bulbous nose. His silver hair was slicked back with gel, giving it a yellow tinge that matched his stained teeth.

"Why *was* Conway chosen as grand marshal?"

"Lots of reasons." Boyle snatched a pack of matches from the unused ashtray on the table, struck one and touched it to the end of his cigarette. He inhaled deeply, tipped his head back, and exhaled a plume of smoke toward the ceiling. "None of them any good."

"Like what?"

"First of all, he's been lobbying to become grand marshal for as long as I've had the misfortune of knowing him. And he's been disrupting our meetings for years."

"Disrupting?"

"Sure, he goes to the committee meetings and starts asking about the parade constitution. You know, when it was written, why no one seems to know anything about it, was there a revision committee, who approved the by-laws? You name it. Accused us on the parade committee of being a bunch of dictators, doing whatever we wanted."

"Why all the fuss?"

"'Cause he was a trouble-maker, that's why, and pushing to be grand marshal. He knew as long as I was parade chairman, he'd make grand marshal over my dead body." Boyle smiled, took a drag on his cigarette and broke into a fit of coughing. When he got his cough under control he added: "Looks like it might turn out to be over *his* dead body."

"So, how *did* he get to be grand marshal?"

"Made an end-run. Claimed he wanted the selection process to be"—Boyle fashioned quotation marks in the air with his fingers—"more democratic. So he enlists the support of some of the other Emerald Societies to gang up against the committee. You might say he played the gay card."

"How's that?"

"Conway knew there were plenty of people who'd do anything to keep the Gay Irish and Lesbian Alliance—GILA—out of the parade."

Danny already knew that Conway's stand against gay marchers was news not only in the Irish community, but had spilled over into the mainstream press as well. Conway had reportedly received death threats, and the parade had been officially boycotted by a consortium of gay groups who held a counter-rally the morning of the 17th on the steps of St. Patrick's Cathedral. As the controversy grew, some members of the Parade Committee had leaked to the press that they regretted their choice of Conway as grand marshal because he'd delighted in fanning the flames of the conflict.

"The committee was divided on whether GILA should be allowed to march," Boyle went on. "Conway made us out to be a bunch of limp wrists and turned half the membership of the Emerald Societies against us."

"Is Conway really that anti-gay?"

Boyle knocked the ashes off the end of his cigarette onto the floor and picked up his Dewar's and water. He took a gulp of his drink, set it down, and smiled at Danny. "Who knows what he really believes. He'll do anything, use any cause to get what he wants. Let's just say he had his own reasons for keeping the gay Irish out of the parade."

"What reasons? Don't they have the same right as anyone else to march in the parade? They're Irish, too."

"The fact is," Boyle said, "the Supreme Court already ruled in our favor on this. We have the legitimate right to exclude any organized group that does not subscribe to the values of our organization."

"Which values?"

"The teachings of the Catholic Church. We're talking about the celebration of a saint's feast day. Let me ask you something. Do you think the Orange Order should be allowed in the parade?''

The Orange Order took its name from William of Orange, whose victory in 1690 at the Battle of the Boyne marked the beginning of Protestant control over Catholics in Ireland. "Of course not," said Danny, "that's ridiculous."

"Why not? Like you say, they're Irish, too. Their members were born in Ireland. So why shouldn't they be allowed to march?'' Boyle didn't wait for Danny to answer. "You know why they shouldn't. Because the Orange Order is fundamentally opposed to everything the St. Patrick's Day parade stands for. They are by their own definition anti-Catholic.''

"But—''

"Any homosexual can march in our parade,'' Boyle cut him off. "We assume many do. But no organization can march under a banner promoting homosexuality as a lifestyle because that lifestyle is in direct opposition to the values of the parade…not to mention Saint Patrick.''

"But Conway—''

"Let me tell you something, kid. Conway has nine children,'' Boyle interrupted again. "Eight girls. That's right—*girls*. They kept trying to have a boy. Finally they did. The ninth kid was a boy—Matt. He's twenty-two years old now.''

"Oh?''

Boyle looked at Danny over the rim of his drink. "He's a dancer.''

Danny waited, watching a sneer develop on the chairman's face, anticipating what Boyle would say.

Boyle cracked an ice cube with his teeth. "He's gay."

"So what?" Danny asked.

"Don't get me wrong," said Boyle, putting down his drink. "Finn loves his boy. Worships him. But I think he takes it as a personal insult the kid turned out light in the loafers."

"So Conway took it out on GILA?"

"Maybe so. He certainly didn't want to see his own son among the gay marchers while he was grand marshal."

"Who else besides himself wanted Conway to be grand marshal?" Danny asked.

"Not me, that's for sure."

"Why not?"

"Finn and I used to be good friends. We even own some vacation property together in Ireland. But it's a given that any grand marshal, from Maureen O'Hara on down, supports a united Ireland."

Danny was well aware that the Irish-American community was noted for being the most militant of the Irish in its desire that all thirty-two counties of Ireland be united one day. "Conway doesn't?"

"Let's just say some of us in the Ancient Order of Hibernians don't think he supports a united Ireland strongly enough. When the leader of *Sinn Fein*, Gerry Adams, was in town, he wasn't even invited to meet Conway, who could have given him a lot better press than he got. You know what *Sinn Fein* is, don't you?"

"Of course." *Sinn Fein* was the political party considered the official wing of the Irish Republican Army.

"Gerry Adams has been president of *Sinn Fein* since nineteen eighty-three," Boyle added. "I sat in this very bar with him when he visited New York for the first time. Conway never even mentioned Gerry's visit in his column. Adams deserves a lot more respect than that."

"You think the attack on Conway had something to do with Northern Ireland politics?"

Boyle took another sip of his Dewar's and water. "Everything in the Irish-American community, including the St. Patrick's Day parade, has to do with Irish politics. I'm not the only one who thinks this Good Friday Agreement is a load of crap."

The agreement signed on Good Friday 1998, Danny recalled, addressed human rights issues, civil rights, policing, and prisoners, and attempted to lay a foundation for peaceful coexistence between Catholics and Protestants in Northern Ireland.

"This so-called power-sharing clause is a hoax," Boyle went on. "*Sinn Fein* wants to share power with those murderers? Why should we share anything with people who have no legitimate claim to Ireland at all? It's a bunch of manure."

The power-sharing clause had been implemented, then called off, then implemented again.

"I don't think most people understand what this Good Friday Agreement has really done."

"What's that?"

"Part of the deal is the Republic of Ireland drops from its constitution its claim to the six counties of the North. That means the Republic recognizes Northern Ireland as a legitimate state. It is *not* a legitimate state! It is a part of Ireland under occupation.

Now they want the IRA to destroy its arms. That's not an agreement. That's surrender. Did Fintan Conway ever say any of that in his columns? No way!''

"And you think someone from the IRA may have shot Conway?''

"Did I say that? Not everyone is happy about this agreement. It could just as easily have been some Protestant terrorist group. Maybe the Red Hand Brigade. After all, he called them scum.''

"But why would any of them shoot Conway? Do you have reason to believe it might have been this Red Hand Brigade?''

Boyle snubbed out his cigarette. "In fact, I do. I think Finn was threatened by those Protestant thugs.''

"Why?''

"Why else would he slander the IRA the way he did? I think the Red Hand, or one of them, put pressure on him.''

"Interesting.''

Boyle lit another cigarette. "But then, to be honest, kid, Conway has hundreds of personal enemies. It could have been any one of them. Someone he insulted in his stupid column years ago, maybe.''

"What about the pro-lifers? I heard he was on one of their lists.''

"I think you're barking up the wrong tree there. It's probably a lot simpler than that. Who knows, maybe it was just a lone, crazy gunman like the papers say.''

In a leprechaun mask? "My buddy Brendan Grady is the guy they're saying did it and he's in a lot of trouble. According to the newspaper, he was in a room in the Plaza Hotel the day Conway was shot.

He won't tell the police why he was in that room, but I don't think he shot Fintan Conway.''

"Is that what he says?" Boyle dragged on his cigarette as if it were life-support, then snubbed it out in the ashtray and lit another. When he dragged on the new one, he coughed a deep gurgling cough as if he were drowning, then took another gulp of his Scotch. "Sounds like he's got something to hide."

"I know he's trying to hide something, but I don't think it's Conway's murder."

"Must be something serious if he's willing to take the rap."

"They say Brendan's prints were found in the room in the Plaza where they believe the shots were fired from. Brendan was picked up at P.J. Carney's on Fifty-Seventh and Seventh a half an hour after the shooting—less than three blocks from the Plaza. Does that sound like something a man would do? Shoot the grand marshal of the St. Patrick's Day parade with a high-powered rifle from a room at the Plaza, then stroll over to Carney's for a pint?"

Boyle's smile revealed a set of yellow teeth. His crooked upper left incisor gleamed. "Depends on how badly he needed a drink."

"Oh, come on."

"All I know is there are hundreds of people who hate Finn Conway enough to shoot him." Boyle picked up his drink and held it midway to his lips. "Guy who did it ought to get a medal."

SEVEN

ON TUESDAY, MARCH 20TH, three days after the shooting, Danny and Fidelma were on their way to Rikers Island.

Driving east across Queens on the Grand Central Parkway, Danny again had a feeling they were being followed. Several times he glanced in his rearview mirror and saw a green Mercedes Benz behind them. He started to say something to Fidelma, but decided not to alarm her. Putting it into words might alarm him, too. Why the heck would they be followed? What had he done to get followed, anyway? When he exited the parkway onto Ditmars Boulevard, the green Mercedes did the same.

Danny's heartbeat quickened. He turned onto Hazen Street, found the parking area for Rikers Island, and swung his Honda Accord into an empty space. The green Mercedes pulled into a parking spot ten spaces from them. No one got out.

It was cool and mostly clear, except for a few cirrus clouds that hung like strips of dirty rags in the sky and a bluish haze of smog that colored the air. Danny and Fidelma boarded the bus that would take them across the bridge to the 415-acre island. The Mercedes disappeared.

As he and Fidelma rode the bus over the only

bridge providing access to Rikers Island, Danny tried to imagine his old friend from the Irish village of Ballycara being locked up there. Brendan was the very first person Danny had met in Ballycara.

Danny remembered as if it were yesterday, the first time he had driven into the village. The main street of the tiny town had been nearly deserted. Danny had stopped his rental car in front of a low building with a neon Harp Lager sign in the window. Then a young man stepped out of the pub and Danny asked for directions.

"So, it's a holiday you're on is it?" Brendan had asked. His Irish accent was so thick Danny could hardly understand him. "When you're settled in, come on over to Larkin's and I'll stand you a pint."

That had been the beginning of a wonderful friendship.

Now it seemed impossible that that beginning had led to Rikers Island—a sprawling urban jail. Rikers sits in the East River off the South Bronx, and less than 1,000 yards from the Hunts Point Sewage Treatment Plant. Housing nearly 20,000 prisoners in ten different jails for men and women, criminals of every type and deed were confined in close, stinking cells—most of them awaiting trial.

Some prisoners, Danny thought—like Brendan Grady—probably didn't belong there at all. Or at least Danny hoped Brendan didn't belong there.

The bridge Danny and Fidelma rode over linked two drastically different worlds. The living, breathing, energetic life of New York City was separated by that bridge from the living death of waiting in the narrow cells of Rikers Island with its ominous address: 1313 Hazen Street.

"I still can't believe this is happening," Fidelma said. "I've known Brendan since we were children. We've got to get him out of here. I know he can't be involved in this."

Danny wanted to believe her, but how could he really be sure? Even in Ireland, Brendan's comings and goings were considered suspicious. Could he sit in a hotel room with a high-powered rifle and shoot Fintan Conway as he marched up 5th Avenue with a *shillelagh* under his arm and his wife by his side? It just did not square with Danny's image of the affable Brendan Grady, cracking jokes over pints of Guinness in Larkin's Pub in Ballycara, but how could he know?

The Intake Facility for visitors was crowded with some forty or fifty men, women, and children waiting to see their loved ones. The roar of voices filled the room. Well-dressed men in suits paced the floor, obviously lawyers there to see clients. Even a priest in his Roman collar stood in line waiting his turn. Danny and Fidelma lined up to show identification, then emptied their pockets. A female Corrections Officer put the contents of their pockets into plastic baskets. Change went into one basket, keys in another. Fidelma put her purse on a conveyor belt that sent it through an X-ray machine. After these necessary formalities they were instructed to take off their shoes.

"Take off our shoes?" Fidelma asked.

"That's what I said," the tough-looking CO shouted above the noise.

If this were a movie, Danny thought, she'd be played by Kathy Bates.

"Why?" asked Fidelma.

"Just hurry up," the CO snapped.

Danny and Fidelma removed their shoes and passed through a metal detector.

The beeper went off as Danny walked through and his pulse raced even though he knew he had nothing to hide. The whole process, the noise inside the prison, the COs, the high security, made him nervous.

"Step over here," said a burly CO. "Hold out your arms."

Danny put out his arms while the guard ran a probe down his sides, beneath his outstretched arms to his armpits and up the insides of his shaking legs.

"Take off your belt."

That too went into a basket.

Danny grabbed his sagging pants as he passed through the detector again. He and Fidelma took back their change and keys with trembling hands. Another Corrections Officer escorted them down a corridor to a visitors room where they bought tepid coffee from a vending machine. They sat there for at least twenty minutes.

"Do you think the guards are making us wait this long to make sure we know who's in control?" Fidelma asked.

"Maybe," Danny said. He also thought that Brendan was probably going through the same ritual on his side.

Another CO took them to a room where chairs had been arranged around dozens of small tables with Formica tops. Danny and Fidelma took a seat. Corrections Officers in each corner of the room watched the forty or fifty waiting people. A booth stood in the center where a CO looked down over the crowd of some twenty other prisoners in identical green jumpsuits already sitting with their visitors at tables scattered throughout the room.

"I hate seeing Brendan like this," said Fidelma.

"You have to," Danny answered. "We're already here."

After another twenty minutes, Brendan was escorted into the room wearing a forest-green jumpsuit and boots, and was brought to one of the small tables.

"No handshakes," said the guard as Danny and Fidelma sat in a chair facing him. "No touching of any kind."

"Danny!" Brendan said, a smile lighting his face. "Fidelma! What are you two doing here?"

Fidelma reached out and took Brendan's hand as if she had not heard the CO's warning. Brendan clutched her slender fingers and did not let them go. The guard turned his back on them and walked away.

Seeing Brendan in here was disorienting. The drab concrete walls, the metal bars, the noise, the indifferent guards, all the security, the body searches, just so he could sit down and have a conversation with his old friend.

"What am *I* doing here?" Danny asked. He started to say, What in God's name are you doing here? But he didn't want to seem too forceful and accusing. He knew why Brendan was in prison. He just hoped it wouldn't be for too much longer. "We're here to help you if we can."

Brendan looked away. In profile, Brendan seemed as though he had aged more than the one year since Danny had last seen him. He had let his Mohawk grow out (it had returned to its natural dark brown) and now wore his hair over his ears. The skin along his jaws and neck sagged slightly and his sideburns and hair were dusted with gray. His bony cheeks and the dark bags under his bloodshot eyes gave him a gaunt and haunted look. Brendan fished a cigarette out of his pocket with shaky fingers and asked the CO standing across the room for a light.

Danny didn't recall that Brendan smoked.

Fidelma sat uneasily at the table, glancing around. Several prisoners watched her hungrily.

Danny didn't know where to begin. "Brendan," he asked, "what made you come to New York?"

"I was playing in a band."

"Why didn't you tell us you were here?" asked Fidelma, gently.

"Oh, I got busy, sure. I was getting around to it."

"What's the name of your group?" Fidelma asked.

"It's not mine. A fellow named Ian Masters is the leader. He hired me to play fiddle. The band's called Dead Leper Cons."

"Celtic rock?" asked Danny.

"More or less."

"You're in a lot of trouble, Brendan." Danny felt stupid as soon as the words were out of his mouth. Slow down, slow down, he said to himself.

"You think I don't know that?"

"You need a lawyer. Fidelma and I can help you get one if you want. I know some good ones in the city."

Fidelma nodded enthusiastically. "We'll do anything we can. I hate seeing you locked up in here like this."

Brendan dropped his head. "I have a solicitor," he mumbled.

"Who is it?"

"Gavin Mallen."

"*The* Gavin Mallen?"

"Who's that?" asked Fidelma.

"Mallen's a New York attorney," Danny explained. "Best known as the U.S. spokesperson for the Thirty-Two County Solidarity Commission." He did not explain that the commission was a group that allegedly funneled funds to the provisional wing of the Irish Republican Army. He decided just to let that go for the moment. "Who's paying for it?" he asked.

"Danny, don't get involved."

"What? I want to help you, Brendan. What about this band? Maybe one of them can provide an alibi for you."

"Leave them out of it."

"Why?"

"You said you'd do anything you can to help me," said Brendan.

"You just tell us," Fidelma said. "Anything."

"All right, you can help me, so."

"How?" Fidelma asked.

"By staying out of this."

"What do you mean stay out of it?" Danny raised his voice.

"Leave off, Dan. My solicitor says I can't talk about any of this."

"Brendan, you better start talking. You could get the death sentence for this."

"Get away from it, Dan."

What in God's name was he thinking? He should be fighting for his life. "You *are* involved, aren't you?" asked Danny.

Brendan looked away.

"If Conway dies," Danny said, "you'll be facing murder in the first degree."

Brendan glanced around, then lowered his voice. "I didn't kill anybody."

"Then for goodness' sake let us help you," Fidelma said.

"You've got to trust me. It's best if you just stay out of this. I can take care of myself."

Danny looked at Brendan for a long time. "Just tell me, Brendan. Did you..." now Danny lowered his voice, "have anything to do with Conway...?"

"I swear to God I had nothing to do with it."

"Do you know who did?"

"No!"

"Then what were you doing at the Plaza Hotel?" Danny asked. "How did you get into the hotel room?"

"The door was unlocked."

"But why? Why were you there?"

"I can't talk about this. Solicitor's orders."

"Okay, Brendan." Danny shook his head. What was he supposed to do? Brendan didn't seem to want any help. Danny dropped his line of questioning. He was here to give his friend support, not badger him. "We're going to stick by you, Brendan."

They talked for another twenty minutes or so until a CO called from across the room, "Time's up."

Danny and Fidelma got up and prepared to leave as another Corrections Officer escorted Brendan away. Just before Brendan left the room, Danny said, "By the way, do you know anybody who drives a green Mercedes Benz?"

Brendan shook his head as he was taken from the room.

EIGHT

AFTER THE BUS RIDE back across the bridge to the Rikers Island parking lot in Queens, Danny and Fidelma returned to their car. Danny glanced around for the green Mercedes. Relieved that it was nowhere in sight, he opened the passenger side for Fidelma, then got behind the wheel of his Honda Accord. Danny kept the car in a garage most of the time and used public transportation. But it came in handy for trips like this or excursions out of the city. Still checking for the Mercedes in his rearview mirror, Danny turned onto Hazen Street. No one seemed to be following as he made a right onto Ditmars Boulevard. Now Danny tried not to glance in the rearview. Instead he checked to make sure he had enough gas, fiddled with the dial on the radio, looked at his watch. But finally he couldn't stop himself. He checked the mirror again.

Fidelma peered at him. "What's wrong?"

"Nothing." Maybe he'd imagined the whole thing. It was probably just coincidence that the car had been behind them before. The whole encounter with Brendan had rattled him. Not just Brendan's reluctance to cooperate, but the atmosphere in the prison left him feeling dispirited.

Another right brought them onto the Grand Central

Parkway. Danny sighed with relief that they weren't being followed. He was just being paranoid.

Fidelma seemed to pick up on his nervousness. "I guess you're worried about Brendan."

"I'm a lot more worried about him than he seems to be about himself."

"We've got to help him."

"He doesn't want our help."

"I don't care what he wants," Fidelma said. "I don't think he realizes how serious this is."

"Oh, he realizes it," said Danny. "He's got Gavin Mallen representing him. Did you know that Mallen is best known for funneling funds to the provisional wing of the IRA?"

"What's that supposed to mean?"

"Nothing. Just wanted to make sure you know who we're dealing with."

"What are you going to do to help Brendan?" Fidelma asked.

"Hey, you're the one who told me not to get involved."

"That was before Brendan was arrested."

"Now everything's different?"

"Of course everything is different!" she said, an edge of hysteria in her voice.

At the tollbooth, Danny handed over three-fifty for the Triboro Bridge and pulled past the booth. Racing along the bridge, they could see to their right the brown, crumbling tenements of Upper Manhattan—Harlem, Morningside Heights, Washington Heights, Inwood—and the gleaming spires of Midtown and Lower Manhattan to the left. As he drove west toward Manhattan, a car raced across three lanes of traffic to exit the parkway, cutting Danny off. "Idiot!" Danny screamed, laying on the horn. "Did you see that guy?"

"Brendan never did say what he was doing at the Plaza Hotel," said Fidelma.

"No, he didn't. But he swears he had nothing to do with shooting Conway."

"Of course he didn't. The police have to find that fellow in the mask."

"Why are you so focused on the mask?"

"Sure, aren't you the one who saw a gun flash in his hand?"

"I didn't say a gun."

"And if you were going to shoot someone at a parade," Fidelma began, "wouldn't it be logical to wear a mask?"

"I wouldn't know, I've never wanted to shoot anyone at a parade…or anywhere else, for that matter."

On the bridge, a green Mercedes pulled up beside Danny and his heart fluttered. But the car was an older model driven by a middle-aged woman who soon passed them. Danny relaxed.

"So, what do you intend to do?" Fidelma asked.

"About what?"

"Danny, they have the death penalty here in America. Brendan could die."

"They haven't executed anyone in New York in years."

Fidelma threw up her hands. "Oh, what a relief. So, you plan to just let Brendan sit there?"

"What do you expect me to do?"

"Something!"

"Fidelma, I'm a high-school teacher. Do you honestly think there is anything I can do about this?"

"You found the murderers of your cousin, Rose,

and of Father O'Malley in Ireland. Why can't you find out who tried to kill Fintan Conway right here in New York?''

As they came off the Triboro Bridge and onto the Harlem River Drive, Danny saw the familiar Mercedes hood ornament on a green car parked beside the Amoco station at the foot of the bridge on 2nd Avenue. As Danny accelerated into uptown traffic on the Harlem River Drive, the car cut across the parking lot of the gas station and took off after him. Danny was sure it was the same one that had followed him earlier. He glanced in the rearview mirror and threw the car into third gear.

"Why are you so nervous?" Fidelma asked.

"I don't like driving."

Danny downshifted and passed the car in front, glanced in the mirror and saw the green Mercedes speed up.

"Danny, I love you," Fidelma said quietly. "You know that."

Danny looked at his speedometer—he was already doing 70—and wondered why Fidelma chose this moment to talk about love.

"But, if you don't help Brendan, then our..." she hesitated as if searching for a word, "well, I'm afraid I won't want to see you anymore."

Danny jerked his head around to her and said incredulously, "What?"

Just then the Mercedes pulled alongside Danny. Four men sat in the car: two in the front and two in the back. The one on the passenger side in front motioned Danny to pull over.

"Who's that?" Fidelma asked.

Danny spotted an exit ramp onto 145th Street, cut

across two lanes of traffic—horns blaring on the cars he cut off—and made for the exit.

Fidelma screamed as she grabbed the dashboard. "What are you doing?"

Danny downshifted, took the exit at excessive speed and nearly hit a homeless woman pushing a shopping cart full of cans and bottles across the street at the foot of the ramp. The green Mercedes gained on him.

"What's gotten into you?"

Danny raced west on 145th Street, running through a yellow light and then a red. "Those men are following us, and I think they want us to pull over. I don't think it's something I should do."

"Who are they?" Fidelma started to turn around but Danny shouted, "Don't look back. Help me navigate."

Just then a garbage truck came out of a side street—

"Watch out!"

—and Danny swerved to avoid it, scraped the side of a parked van and ripped its side-view mirror off. The mirror skittered onto the sidewalk and shattered against a wall. Danny glanced in his rearview mirror but didn't see the Mercedes.

"I think we lost them," he said. Then he saw the car racing toward them out of a side street. Danny wrenched the wheel to the left, ran up on the sidewalk, sent a garbage can sailing into the plate glass window of a grocery store, and raced the wrong way up a one-way street, turned onto St. Nicholas Avenue and sped uptown.

"Who are these people?" Fidelma asked breathlessly. Her face had lost its color and she gripped the dashboard so hard her fingers were turning purple.

"I wish I knew," he said as he ran through a red light and shot between two cabs. At 155th Street he turned right and made for the highway. Danny got onto the Harlem River Drive, and after five minutes speeding north felt certain he had lost the Mercedes.

"They nearly killed us!"

Near the northern tip of Manhattan the Harlem River Drive makes a Y. To the left is Dyckman Street and to the right is Tenth Avenue. Danny chose to go left. Even though he could have gone right to the University Heights Bridge, crossed the Harlem River, and gotten onto the Major Deegan Expressway, Danny figured anybody following him would assume that's exactly what he'd do. So he drove straight up Dyckman toward Broadway.

Danny sped up Dyckman, which buzzed with pedestrians. Vendors sold flowers from shopping carts and fried foods from makeshift sidewalk stands. Men sat on overturned plastic milk crates slapping dominos down on broken tables while other groups of men and women stood on the corners shuffling to *merengue* music. Danny passed a stalled car, glanced in his rearview mirror again and saw the Mercedes two blocks behind him.

"Dammit!" He wrenched the wheel to the right onto Vermilyea Avenue, scattering a group of kids playing stickball in the street, and roared through a stop sign at Academy.

"What do they want?" Fidelma asked, still gripping the dashboard.

"I don't know."

"They've been following us ever since Rikers, haven't they?" Fidelma asked.

"Yeah. I didn't want to scare you, so I didn't say anything. Besides, I wasn't sure I was right."

"I saw them long before we got to Rikers," Fidelma said. "I didn't say anything because I didn't want to scare *you*."

"Really? How could you see them?"

"I was watching in the side-mirror."

If Danny could just get to his apartment, ditch the car somehow, he and Fidelma could stay there until these people left.

As he bore left onto 204th Street and raced toward Broadway, he glanced in the mirror thinking that at last he had lost them. But as he squeezed the car between two city buses, he saw the green Mercedes speed up 204th in his direction.

Danny threw the car into second gear and sped up Broadway, squealed through a red light, and turned onto 207th Street, two blocks from home.

"Be careful," Fidelma yelled as they raced downhill on 207th.

Suddenly, Danny saw the alley between his building and the adjacent one where the Super stacked the garbage.

"Watch out!" Fidelma screamed as Danny wrenched the wheel to the left.

He had miscalculated his speed and the tires screamed as he fishtailed into the alley, snapping off the mirror on the passenger side as the car scraped against the building, throwing sparks. He slammed on the brakes and came to an abrupt halt, sending two cans of garbage flying.

"Jesus, Mary, and Joseph," Fidelma gasped, blessing herself.

In the rearview mirror, Danny saw the green Mercedes fly past.

NINE

As soon as they got upstairs into the apartment, Danny called Detective Washington. The detective said he'd be at the 19th Precinct station waiting for him.

When Danny arrived at the station, the cop was sitting at his desk flipping through an album of photographs that looked like they may have been taken at the St. Patrick's Day parade.

"Someone's trying to kill me," Danny said immediately, still rattled from the chase.

"Is that so?"

"These people in a green Mercedes Benz have been following me since yesterday. This afternoon they chased me all the way from Rikers Island."

Washington closed the album, leaned back in his chair, and laced his fingers behind his head. "What were you doing going to Rikers?"

"I went to see a friend of mine."

"Who?"

"Brendan Grady."

Washington put his hands down, picked up a pen from his desk and scribbled something on a pad. "So you know the guy who shot Fintan Conway?"

"Brendan didn't whack anybody. I want to find out who did."

Detective Washington laughed. "You want to find out who did? That's a good one. So does the entire New York police force." He picked up a file folder on his desk. "We've done some checking on you since you gave your statement."

Danny looked surprised. "On me?"

"You solved a couple crimes in Dear Old Ireland." Washington's imitation of an Irish accent fell flat.

"That's right."

"Now you want to find out who shot Fintan Conway in one of the biggest cities in the world? This ain't Ballycarmen."

"Ballycara," Danny corrected.

Washington pointed his ballpoint at Danny. "You remind me of one of those characters in an Agatha Christie novel. You know, little mustache, umbrella. Solves crimes by sitting around in an armchair *ruminating*."

"You read Agatha Christie?"

"I seen it on PBS," Washington muttered, opening the file folder. "Now let me get this straight: You nailed the guy who killed your cousin, Rose Noonan, by using genealogical research?"

Several years ago Danny had gone to Ireland to research his roots. Unfortunately, when he arrived, he had found his cousin bludgeoned to death in her vegetable garden. The weapon used had been a turf spade. Danny was the chief suspect. To clear his name, he had to show how the roots of his own past were entwined with the death of his cousin Rose.

"That's right."

Washington turned over one of the pages in the folder. "And you solved the murder of a priest by using some hocus pocus with Rosary beads?"

Last year, Danny's good friend in Ireland, Father O'Malley, had said 7:30 Mass. Afterward, the priest failed to return to the rectory. This was so uncharacteristic of him that Fidelma, who was the cleric's housekeeper at the time, was sure something had happened. Garda Kelley, the village policeman, was on vacation in Spain. Fidelma had asked Danny to see if he could find the priest. He did find him—dead.

"Not exactly. But close enough," said Danny.

Washington closed the file folder. His bloodshot eyes bulged and a vein in his neck throbbed. "Let me tell you a few of the facts of life, O'Flaherty. You want to know how crimes are *really* solved? By dedicated, hardworking men and women from the police department working around the clock preserving the crime scene, collecting evidence, making notes, photographs, sketches, measurements, fingerprints, DNA fingerprinting, earprint identification. That's right, *earprint* identification! Ever heard of that? Forensics, O'Flaherty, forensics! Forensic dentistry, bone identification, autopsies, bloodstain evidence, hair analysis." Washington leaned back, exhausted. "That's the real world, pal, where perps get sent to prison based on evidence. We don't gather the suspects in the library at the end of the day and announce the butler done it."

"I never said you did."

"So, while you mull over Conway's attempted murder in your armchair, dedicated, underpaid, underappreciated, over-worked professionals are out there working the crime. It's called procedure. Don't get in the way of it."

Danny drummed his fingers on the detective's desk.

"Now, I don't suppose you bothered to notice what kind of Mercedes was tailing you?"

"A Calypso Green C280."

Washington whistled through his teeth and set down his pen. He made a cathedral of his fingers and examined Danny with an amused expression. "Well my, my, my. How observant. Calypso green, huh?"

"That's right. I stopped at a dealership on the way down here and found the exact same model and color. They call it Calypso Green."

Washington chewed on that for a moment. "Okay. What else you got?"

Danny told Washington everything he could about the four men in the car. "They were all in their late thirties, I'd say. Except the driver was maybe closer to fifty."

The detective seemed to have calmed down and he took notes on what Danny told him.

"You think maybe they saw you talking to the police at the parade?" Washington asked. "Been following you ever since?"

"I don't know, maybe."

Then Washington questioned Danny in detail about the four men and the car. Later, as Danny got up to leave, Washington added, "Now, I'll give *you* something, O'Flaherty."

"Yeah?"

"Only way to put the finger on whoever shot Conway is by using forensics. You got that? To begin with your story about something flashing in the masked person's hand is full of holes."

"Why?"

"If your leprechaun was shooting a silenced pistol, you wouldn't see any flash from the weapon. Silencers work by diffusing escaping gases, so that would absorb any flame.''

"But it might have been the sun glinting off the barrel.''

Washington popped a breath mint into his mouth and talked around it. "It's all frigging forensics, O'Flaherty.''

"Solving murders is about stories,'' said Danny quietly.

"Say what?''

"I said solving murders is about listening to stories. The victim has one. Everybody who knew the victim has one. You have a story. I have a story. I believe if you listen, you'll find out how and where the killer's story intersected with the victim's.''

"Is that so?''

"You know,'' said Danny. "I'm curious about *your* story.''

"You want a story, O'Flaherty?'' Washington asked. "I'll give you a good one. Long time ago, before I made detective, I'm working with this guy Bobby McCarthy—one of you Irish guys—we're radio car cops. We get a call around midnight. Tells us to meet the detectives at Hundred and Eighty-First and Broadway, somebody's squirtin' metal in an apartment building up there.''

"Squirtin' metal?''

"Shooting the place up. We get up there, the first thing we see is an ambulance and they're carrying bodies down from upstairs. We get up to the fourth floor with about a dozen other cops to this apartment, turns out to be a base house for a crack operation. Some jingle-brain goes in there with an Uzi and a plan for quick riches. Don't ask me how he gets in with a weapon because those places are usually guarded like Fort Knox. Anyway, he goes in there and starts shooting up the place. Well, me and Bobby had seen some things before but nothing like this. By the time we get to the third floor there's a river of blood pouring down the stairs. Inside the apartment there's blood and guts all over the place—a half dozen dead men and women just blown to pieces, including the Einstein who decided to rob a crack house.''

"Sounds horrible," Danny whispered.

"That ain't the half of it. Me and Bobby, we're walking around with body parts up to our knees. We open the bathroom door. The bathtub's overflowing with blood and water. There's a woman dead in the tub.''

"My God.''

"That's when I see the rubber duck." Washington paused. When he spoke again his voice was faint. "I had two kids in my house at the time. A three-year-old and a newborn." Washington looked at a point over Danny's left shoulder. "We found a baby floating in the bath. Woman was giving her baby a bath—yeah, in the crack house. Don't ask…" Washington couldn't finish the sentence.

Danny put on his jacket. "Thanks for your help, Detective.''

TEN

THE NEXT NIGHT—Wednesday, March 21st—was gusty and cold. A raw wind clawed at Danny's face as he wrapped his scarf around his neck, pulled his tweed cap lower on his head, and made his way from the subway to O'Dwyer's Pub in the Bainbridge section of the Bronx.

Bainbridge Avenue and 204th Street are the crossroads for the newly-arrived Irish immigrants of New York. It is a mixed area of Spanish bodegas and Irish grocery stores selling rashers, bangers, and Irish soda bread. There were a few diners where you could still get an Irish breakfast and newsstands that sold Irish newspapers. O'Dwyer's was one of a dozen Irish pubs, like Blackthorne's, The Green Isle, O'Gorman's, in the area of Bainbridge and 204th.

Danny pushed his way through the dark, smoky interior and found a place at the bar. The pub had seen better days and it was the kind of place that when a stranger, like Danny, walked in, a hush fell over the drinkers and everyone watched him sit down. Paintings of Irish cottages hung behind the cash register. One picture of a crumbling cottage pasted to a cabinet behind the bar was labeled "ancestral home of the O'Dwyers."

The bartender stood beneath a pair of crossed hurley-sticks. He didn't look particularly pleased to see Danny. "What do you want?"

"Pint of Harp."

Danny turned on his barstool and checked out Brendan Grady's band. Dead Leper Cons consisted of a fiddle player, a drummer playing a goatskin drum called a *bodhrán,* an *uilleann* pipes player, an electric guitar, a bass guitar and a lead singer with a voice like a worn brake shoe.

Danny sipped his Harp as the band worked through its set. The music blended Irish traditional and punk rock—a hybrid known as Celtic rock. Its beat was hard-driving with the screaming lead guitar riffs of acid rock, but the fiddle and *uilleann* pipes embroidered it with a thread of lyrical poetry that softened its rough edges.

> Screw this dreary island
> With its rain, rain, rain.
> Shove the stars and shamrocks
> Gimme pain, pain, pain.

Dead Leper Cons worked through three more edgy numbers, then stopped suddenly and put down their instruments.

"Good sound," Danny said to the lead singer, who walked up to the bar. "Buy you a drink?"

"Thanks, mate. They're on the house. Only decent thing about this bloody gig." He motioned to the bartender. "Pint and a Paddy."

The barman pulled a pint of Guinness and poured a shot of Paddy Old Irish Whiskey.

The singer had the look of a man who had been three weeks straight without sleep. There were acne scars along his jawbones and neck that a thin beard did little to hide. His long dishwater blond hair was pulled away from his bony face in a ponytail and his watery blue eyes looked out through droopy lids. He wore a silver skull and bones on his left ear and a gold ring through his right eyelid.

"Could I ask you a few questions?"

The singer studied Danny. "Who're you?" he asked in a hard-edged, Belfast burr. "Immigration?"

"Friend of Brendan Grady's."

"Look, mate. I don't know nothing 'bout his troubles. All I know's he's up to his *arse* in alligators."

Indeed, he was. Was that something they said in Belfast? "I'm trying to help him," Danny said.

"Well, I've given all the help I can. The cops came to my apartment day before yesterday and I told them everything I know. And I mean everything. They wanted to know when and where I was born, who my *associates* are, where my parents live, who my friends are, which hand I use to wipe my..."

"I get the idea."

"Why would Brendan want to bump off that old guy Conway?"

"I don't think he did."

"You don't say." The singer shot back the jigger of whiskey, took a deep gulp of his stout, belched loudly, and fished in his shirt pocket for a cigarette.

"Can you tell me when the last time you saw Brendan was?"

"Sure. He was here with us on the sixteenth. We finished up about one a.m. The rest of us stayed around after chucking out time drinking pints, but he ran off like he'd somewheres important to go. Then, of course, he never showed at all on St. Paddy's. We played that night without a fiddle and it bloody stank. Then we found this new fiddle player yesterday. Not as good as Brendan, but he'll do."

"How well did you know Brendan?"

"Hardly a-tall. He's a *culchie*. A hick, as you Yanks say, from some Ballybumfook village in the Republic."

"Look," Danny said, his pulse quickening. "Brendan's in a lot of trouble."

"That he is." The singer raised his pint. "My sympathies. He'll be fiddling for the niggers in the chokey looks like."

Danny felt like grabbing this guy by his long hair and smashing his face against the mahogany bar. "He's a good friend," he said evenly.

"He should have stayed down on the farm."

"What's your name?" Danny asked.

The singer polished off his stout and signaled for another. "Who wants to know?"

"My name's O'Flaherty..." Danny put out his hand. "Danny O'Flaherty."

The singer stared at the hand but did not shake it. "Name's Ian Masters. Remember it. It's gonna be big."

"I'm sure."

Ian flicked his thumb at the tiny bandstand crammed into a corner of the room that was mostly taken up by a pool table. "I'm on to better things than this sewer, I can assure you. I've got a recording contract with Black Crow Records."

"Yeah, well, before you leave for Carnegie Hall, is there anything you remember that Brendan did or said that night before St. Patrick's Day that seemed unusual?"

"Far as I'm concerned, everything he did and said was unusual."

"How so?"

"Like I told you, he was a *culchie,* but I think he played the cloak and dagger games to make himself look important."

"What cloak and dagger games?"

"Ah, sure, the rushing here and there like he had somewheres to go. Now he could play the fiddle, I'll not deny that. But could he be relied on? Well, he left us high and dry on St. Paddy's Day."

Ian chugged down his pint, and Danny thought: You haven't been dry in ages, pal. "That's it?"

"Far as I'm concerned, that's it and that's the end of it," said Ian. "It's no concern o'mine."

"What if Brendan is convicted of a murder he didn't commit?"

"What makes you so sure he *didn't* shoot your man Conway?"

Danny paused and took a sip of his Harp. What *did* make him so sure? After all, how well did he really know Brendan? They'd had good times together in Ireland at Larkin's Pub. And Brendan had helped Danny find the body of poor Desmond Conlon in the sea off County Clare. But Danny knew nothing of Brendan's comings and goings either in Ireland or New York. He remembered that back in Ireland Brendan was rumored to have ties to the IRA. His family had been militant Republicans for generations. His Uncle Jack had been put in the notorious Long Kesh jail during the civil rights movement in Belfast during the 1960s. Brendan was known to disappear for weeks at a time with no explanation. The bartender at Larkin's Pub in Bally-cara had once said to Brendan, "Didn't your family have a bit of a quarrel with Danny O'Flaherty's grand-father?''

Brendan Grady had made a motion toward the pub-lican to shut him up, but the bartender had raised his voice. ''Sure, didn't it have something to do with your bloody Republican principles?''

Brendan had finally admitted that when the treaty was signed in 1921 creating the Free State of Ireland, leaving the six counties of the North to Britain, those satisfied with the treaty supported the newly-formed Republic of Ireland. But the Irish Republican Army insisted that they would never stop fighting until *all* of Ireland was free.

''Your grandfather,'' Brendan had pointed his fin-ger at Danny, ''sided with the Free Staters and my grandfather died in the glorious service of the IRA.''

Danny took another sip of his Harp and decided to change tack with Ian Masters. ''The last time you saw Brendan you said he rushed out of here?''

''That's right.''

''He didn't say where he was going?''

''No.''

''Did he get a cab? Subway?'' Danny asked.

''Not a bit of it. A car came for him.''

Danny's head snapped up out of his pint. ''Re-ally?''

''Yeah, I was sitting over there with the band.'' Ian pointed to a booth under a window with a green neon shamrock in it overlooking the street. ''It was raining a bit and I happened to look out as Brendan left the pub. I saw him run across the street to that car park over there.''

Danny took another sip of Harp. ''Yeah?''

''Just then a car comes from that direction and its

lights shine on Brendan as he gets into the back seat of a car. Truth be told, I was surprised. I figured he was walking or taking the train—certainly not getting into a car like that.''

''Like what?'' Danny asked.

''A brand new Mercedes,'' said Ian. ''A green Mercedes Benz.''

ELEVEN

IT WAS DRIZZLING SLIGHTLY and Danny could see the faint smoke of his breath in the air as he left the bar. The slick streets shimmered with reflected light and the moan of distant sirens echoed among the buildings. He pulled his topcoat around him, hailed a cab, and crossed the University Heights Bridge into upper Manhattan. Constantly on edge now, he turned several times to see if the green Mercedes might be following but it was too dark to tell.

Who were these people, anyway? Brendan had been seen with them the day before St. Patrick's Day. Maybe this whole thing about the person in the mask was just Danny hanging onto some hope that Brendan was not involved. But he did see something flash in the masked man's hand. The sunlight glinting on a gun, perhaps. Now it seemed that maybe Brendan *did* have something to do with the shooting of Fintan Conway.

Danny stopped at the Piper's Kilt on Broadway near 207th Street for a hamburger. The dining area was full—a fifteen minute wait—so Danny ate his burger standing at the bar with a mug of Coke. Televisions suspended above both ends of the bar broadcast the 11:00 news and Danny watched, hoping for some new development in the St. Patrick's Day shooting. Fintan Conway was still in intensive care after four days.

Danny, of course, had read the newspapers and watched every TV report he could catch, devouring every scrap of information he could on the case. Yesterday, after he met with Detective Washington, he had called some people in the neighborhood who would have known Conway. Bill Cooney, who now owned the O'Flaherty Funeral Parlor, had known Fintan Conway for years.

"Well, sure, he had loads of enemies," Bill had told Danny. "But then again, he had loads of friends."

"Anybody who might have hated him enough to shoot him?"

"It seems to me," Bill had said, "that it was a professional job. Did you know that Finn wrote a column about Mickey Featherstone that nearly got him killed?"

"Mickey Featherstone of the Westies?"

The Westies was an Irish Mob that controlled Manhattan's Hell's Kitchen throughout the '60s, '70s, and '80s.

"Their name was never really the Westies. I don't know how that got started," said Bill. "Their real name was the Coonan Crew. Finn wrote a pretty nasty column about them and there were threats on his life. But that was years ago and the Coonan Crew is mostly a thing of the past. But who knows? There might be some of them still around with an axe to grind."

Danny had also talked to the security guards who had worked at the Plaza Hotel on St. Patrick's Day. Police detectives had searched the Plaza and found

Brendan Grady's fingerprints on a twelfth-floor room overlooking 5th Avenue.

"The room was registered to a tourist from Holland," one of the security guards had told Danny. "The cops questioned and released him."

"But what prompted the police to search the Plaza in the first place?"

"An anonymous tip," the guard had said. But he offered little more.

On the TV over the bar, *New York 1 News* went through its litany of crime and sports stories, city politics, weather, and business. When Danny finished his burger deluxe and motioned for the check, the news anchor said, "This just in," and she picked up the sheet in front of her.

Her eyes darted over the release, then she looked up to the camera and rearranged her features into a grave expression. "Just ten minutes ago, at St. Luke's-Roosevelt Hospital, grand marshal of this year's St. Patrick's Day parade, Fintan Patrick Conway, died of gunshot wounds sustained in the brutal attack against him on the seventeenth of this month."

"Hear that?" asked the elderly woman sitting next to Danny nursing a Vodka Collins. "Poor Finn Conway's dead, God rest his soul."

Another patron listening to the report shouted, "I wouldn't put it past one of those pro-life fanatics to do something like this after what Conway wrote a couple weeks ago. I heard he was put on one of their Internet website death-list things."

"Pro-life, me arse," said a man with an Irish brogue who stood squashed against the bar nursing a boilermaker. "It's as likely the IRA plugged him for all the t'ings he's been saying about them. The IRA don't like to be told they should destroy their arms.''

"Could have been a Loyalist terrorist group," the bartender said. "He called the lot of them scum."

"Well, I heard that GILA group was hopping mad that he opposed homosexual marchers in the parade," the old woman with the Vodka Collins said to Danny. She took a sip from her drink. "And isn't that a shame. Sure, they've the same right to march on St. Patrick's Day as anyone else. The gay groups march in the parade in Dublin. Why shouldn't they do the same in New York?''

"Fairies," the man next to her muttered. Danny knew he wasn't talking about leprechauns. It was just like the Irish to take something as simple as a parade and turn it into internecine bickering, not to mention murder.

"I hardly think," Danny put in, fearing the conversation was veering recklessly toward bigotry, "that anyone would shoot Conway because they weren't allowed to march in the parade."

"Who knows."

"A contradictory man and a controversial choice for grand marshal," the anchor went on, "Fintan Conway will be remembered by his widow and nine surviving children as an Irish boy who came to New York in nineteen fifty-five and made the city his own. He carved out a reputation at the *New York Voice* and made a name for himself in community activism and finally as a columnist."

So now Brendan Grady faced murder in the first degree.

"An illegal Irish immigrant has been arrested in connection with the St. Patrick's Day shooting," the anchor read from her script. "But police believe that a second gunman wearing a mask may have also been involved in what might have been a conspiracy to murder the grand marshal."

When the news was over, Danny paid his check and went to the public phone at the far end of the bar near the door. He dialed the home number of his Aunt Bertie who worked for the Chief Medical Examiner of the City of New York.

"Well," his aunt said jovially, "a blast from the past."

Although Aunt Bertie was over 60 years old, she spoke like a teenager, smoked imported clove cigarettes, wore orange lipstick, and her clothing—she favored bright cotton sundresses and saris, turquoise pendants, gold ear-bangles and multi-colored beads—raised eyebrows in the family. They said she must be related to the Irish Gypsies. "It's not often I hear from my nephew. What do you want this time?"

"Bert," Danny said, "you know I'm busy. Sorry I haven't called."

"Oh, yes. How's school? Still trying to save the world?"

"You know what the school system's like. If I don't help these kids, nobody else will."

"Saint Danny!"

"Give it a rest."

"Listen, Danny, you know one of my dearest friends is a principal at a good school on Long Island."

Here we go again, he thought. His aunt was always trying to get him into a suburban school where the pay was higher and the classes were not combat zones.

"Why won't you at least go talk to her? I'm sure there'll be openings in the fall."

"I like my school," Danny lied. What he really meant was he liked the kids. Most of them had been abandoned by so many people—fathers, mothers, the city itself. Danny didn't have the heart to abandon them, too.

"Where are you?"

"Piper's Kilt."

"Well, good for you. It's about time you got out of that stuffy apartment and had some fun. I hope you're not carrying a stack of papers to grade like usual. Are you dating anyone these days?"

Danny groaned, already regretting having to call Bertie, who always tried to get him a new job and then grilled him on his love life.

"Yes. You met Fidelma."

"Ah, yes. She's a cute one. Are you getting any?"

"Bertie!" Danny parried subjects he didn't want to discuss for a bit longer until he finally got to the point. "I'm wondering if you might do me a favor, Aunt Bertie."

"I knew you wanted something."

"Now, Bert, don't make it sound so mercenary."

"Did I use that word? Come to think of it, I'm not sure I even know what it means."

"Listen, I'm trying to find out what happened to Fintan Conway."

"He died. I just heard it on the news," she said.

"I know he *died*. I'm trying to find out who killed him."

Bertie burst into guffaws. "You're trying to find out? The mayor and the police commissioner have a twelve-man special task force headed by Homicide

Detective George Washington working around the clock sifting through leads and *you're* trying to find out who killed him? Tell me another one!''

Because his aunt worked in the Office of the Chief Medical Examiner of the City of New York, she prided herself on her insider knowledge of city affairs. Danny, however, was stung by the criticism. ''Listen,'' he said defensively, ''an amateur can do a lot of things the police can't.''

''Oh, yeah, like what?''

''Well…like…I don't have to go by police regulations and procedures. I can talk to anyone any time I want. No search warrants.''

''Oh, wow. Planning to kick some doors down, are you?''

''Sifting through leads,'' Danny muttered. ''That's the way the police work—methodically, painstakingly. How creative. Where does intuition come in?''

''It doesn't. It's about evidence, Danny. And about getting a conviction once the evidence is brought to court.''

''They might just miss the forest for the trees. That's where intuition comes in. Besides, the police are spending most of their time gathering background. I've lived in this neighborhood my whole life. I know more about people like Fintan Conway than they ever will.''

''Okay, Sherlock,'' Aunt Bertie said. ''I know you've had some luck with your sleuthing in Ireland, but in case you haven't noticed this is New York City.'' She sounded just like Washington. ''So what is it you want?'' she asked.

''A favor.''

"Well, if it has to do with finding who killed Finn Conway, I suppose I owe *him* a favor."

"What do you mean?"

"It was Finn Conway who got me my job."

"In the coroner's office?"

"That's right. When I was out of work after my midlife crisis…"

Oh, yes, Danny thought. Is that what she's calling it now—a midlife crisis? The family just thought Aunt Bertie had gone nuts. Danny remembered the time she'd holed up on the roof, feeding birds and claiming she wouldn't come down because the birds needed her. She slept on the roof for one night until Danny's father and his Uncle Owen talked her down. Then there was the time years ago when Danny's parents and his brothers and sisters all went to a lodge in the Catskills with Aunt Bertie and Uncle Owen. The whole family had gone down to the lake for a swim, but Aunt Bertie said she was going to take sun on the front yard of the lodge. When the family came back from swimming, Danny noticed a commotion in front of the lodge where a crowd had gathered. Uncle Owen had looked around nervously.

"What's everybody pointing at, Daddy?" Danny's little brother had asked.

When they got back to the lodge, there was Aunt Bertie, stretched out face-up on a lounge chair taking sun without a stitch of clothes on. The owners of the lodge said theirs was a "family" place and the O'Flahertys checked out sheepishly and went back to the city.

"Yes…I think I remember," Danny began.

"You know damn good and well what I'm talking about. Anyway, Owen suggested I talk to Conway. I asked Finn if he could help me. He used his connections with the city and in less than a month I had the job in the coroner's office. Good God, it's nearly twenty years now.''

Danny was amazed by how far-reaching Conway's influence had been.

"So what can I do?"

"I expect there will be an autopsy," Danny said nonchalantly.

"Now wait a minute."

"I'd just like to see a copy of the report."

"Danny, that's impossible. Those reports are confidential—totally confidential."

"Come on, Bert."

"I could lose my job."

"You owe your job to Conway," he said.

"It's unethical."

"Please!"

"It's totally out of the question," Bertie answered with finality.

"Just this once."

"I'm not making any promises."

Danny left the restaurant and went home to his apartment and cat to grade the papers from the test he'd given the class earlier that day.

TWELVE

FIVE MINUTES before the bell was to ring ending class on Thursday, March 22nd, Danny opened his briefcase and began handing back exams. "Soto, Clarey, Hijueles," Danny called as he held up each student's test and handed it back. Danny was relieved to have the week nearly over with. He looked forward to his date with Fidelma in the evening. They were going to see a play. "I'm curving the grades," he announced to the class. "Because if I hadn't, half of you would have failed. Bowers, Burgos, Chen." Danny continued to hand out papers. When he called "Rodriguez," he felt a twinge of disappointment.

When Joey Rodriguez glanced at his exam, a stricken expression clouded his features. Danny saw Joey's eyes moisten, but the look immediately evaporated, replaced by a hard-edged smirk and a tightening of the muscles in Joey's jaws. He certainly wasn't going to let on how hard the failing grade affected him.

The boy swaggered toward the garbage can beside Danny's desk. "I don't need this crap," he mumbled, balling up the exam and pitching it toward the can, missing. "I'm out of here soon."

"Pick that up," Danny said. Then he held up another paper. "McManus."

The bell rang.

"Joey," Danny called, "come here. I want to talk to you."

Joey stood in front of him, the balled-up test in his hand. He wore a hooded sweatshirt, and he crossed his arms defiantly over his chest. A red bandanna was knotted sideways on his head in the style of the Bloods. Or was it the Crips? The laces on his Timberland boots were undone and his trousers were so enormous it looked as if they'd fall off at any minute. "Yo, Teach."

"Did you study?"

"Study what?"

"For the test, Joey, the test."

"Who gives a damn about a bunch of farmers starving to death two hundred years ago?"

Danny started to call him on his language but decided not to go there. "More like one hundred and fifty years."

"Whatever."

"I want you to rewrite the essay question."

"What?"

"Open book. But instead of a half page answer I want a three-page typed essay on the causes of the Irish Potato Famine."

"Oh, man, I—"

"By tomorrow," Danny added. "You're going to pass this class whether you want to or not."

"That ain't fair."

Danny removed his glasses, kneaded his throbbing temples then put his glasses back on. "Like my sweet Irish grandmother used to say, 'Life ain't fair.' Besides, since when is a second chance not fair? What's the matter with you, Joey?"

"Ain't nothing the matter with me, man, 'cept you." Joey squared his shoulders and looked down at Danny. At nearly six-three, he was taller than his teacher, muscular, with a mustache sprouting on his upper lip.

"Is there something I can help you with?"

"Don't need your help. And don't gimme any of that father crap."

"Who said anything about a father?"

Joey was speechless for a moment, then mumbled something Danny didn't catch, but he waited while Joey squeaked the toe of his boot on the floor. "Had to take care of my little sisters," he said.

"I know you have a lot to do at home," Danny said, putting his hand on Joey's shoulder.

Joey shrugged, knocking Danny's hand off. "That's right, I do."

"You're doing a good job, I'm sure. It's an important job."

"Is it?" Joey asked mockingly.

"You have a lot more potential than you're showing, Joey. You're a smart kid."

Joey just looked at him with a bored expression.

"Look, Joey. Let me put it to you this way. You barely passed last semester. We're already into the second marking period and you're failing. Unless you get to work you won't graduate. What are you planning to do with your life?"

"That's my business."

"Let me tell you something, Joey. Those bums you're hanging with under the subway tracks are going to be dead before they're thirty. Is that what you want, too?"

When Joey said nothing, Danny went on. "The

way things look right now I see two doors of opportunity open to you. One is jail and the other is Mickey D's...Mac & Don's Steak House...whatever you want to call it. Flipping burgers.''

"Maybe."

"There's a third way...the Army. Well, let me tell you, not even the Army wants you without a high school diploma or at least a GED."

"I'm gonna be a rapper."

"Give me a break."

"You know how much Puff Daddy made last year?"

"Sean Combs is one in a million, Joey."

"I can be, too."

Danny took a deep breath. Except for the one year on the teacher exchange program in Dublin, he had taught Uptown for all fifteen years of his teaching career. He had seen students like Joey come and go. Most found respectable jobs after graduation. Some had gone on to college. A few had even come back to shake Danny's hand and thank him for his help and encouragement. "You better start studying, Joey."

"Don't worry about me."

But too many of Danny's former students—the ones he still saw nearly every day—were bag boys selling pot on street corners, drinking from quart bottles of Midnight Thunder. Some had already lost the battle with crack cocaine. Others were dead. Danny just didn't want Joey to join the addicted or the dead. "Have you thought at all about what you're going to do when you graduate?"

"I've thought some."

"Any ideas?" If Danny could just make him see

how decisions he made today—even the decision to study or not study for a test—could have an impact on the rest of his life. But how could you make a kid like Joey understand that? Kids were more interested in what their peers thought of them today than what might happen to them when they graduated high school.

"Not really," Joey said.

"Like I said, you better start working. You need to pass my class to graduate and you need to graduate to get a decent job or to get into the Army."

Danny truly wanted to believe what he told Joey. But sometimes he couldn't help thinking that the drug dealers down on the street were probably making a lot more than he was—more than many teachers in the city, most likely. The operative word was *good* job.

"You really gonna make me write this paper?"

Teenagers lived in the here and now, thought Danny. Unfortunately, the here and now was a dangerous and sometimes frightening place. Those who had survived adolescence could look back, like Danny, on the crazy things they had done as kids and laugh. In Danny's day those crazy things could get you in trouble. But the neighborhood was a different world than the one he and Joey's mother had grown up in. Today those crazy things could get you killed.

"I'm giving you a chance, Joey. Don't blow it." What else could he tell him right now? What else could he do but try to set an example and try to hold Joey to the same standard he held the rest of his students? "It's cold out there."

Joey shrugged. "I know how to take care of myself," he said as he strode to the door.

Danny hoped so.

THIRTEEN

DANNY AND FIDELMA had reserved seats for the Thursday evening performance of *Everything I Know About the Irish I Learned at McSorley's* by Francis McCormick—whose memoir of growing up poor in Cork, *Anger's Ashcan,* had rocketed to the top of the *New York Times* best-seller list. A fixture on the New York Irish scene for years, McCormick found himself the darling of the media, a role he obviously relished, and was completing a second volume of his memoirs entitled *'Twill.* The play was at the Irish Repertory Theatre on West 22nd Street in Manhattan. The theatre, as Danny told Fidelma when he picked up the tickets at the box office, was founded in 1988 by Ciaran O'Reilly and Charlotte Moore and boasted "a company of over one hundred performers and designers specializing in staging works by outstanding Irish and Irish-American playwrights."

Fidelma said he sounded like a guidebook.

Fintan Conway had been on the Board of Directors of the Irish Repertory when he'd been killed, and Danny wanted to hear what Conway's son had to say at the memorial scheduled before the performance.

Before the curtain rose on McCormick's play, an emcee asked that a prayer be said for Fintan Conway, and silence fell over the auditorium. Then Conway's son was introduced. Fintan Conway II, a dancer in the New York production of *Dance of the River Lord,* had renamed himself Matt Gill to distance himself from his notorious father (some claimed), or to flatten the ethnicity of his name. A swath of Matt's straight black hair fell across his forehead and he swept it away with a delicate hand. He wore white cotton slacks and a blue silk shirt open in front, revealing a gold chain twinkling among the hair on his chest. A diamond stud glittered on his left ear. He stood and gave a half-hearted speech of thanks for remembering his father.

To Danny's surprise, a former student of his from the neighborhood, Aileen Fannon, was in one of the leading roles of the production. He remembered Aileen as a class clown who had not only made the class laugh, but Danny as well, despite himself. So she made it out of the 'hood, Danny thought.

The show was a lively and entertaining summary in song and dance of the Irish in early New York from the seventeenth century to just before the time of the Civil War. Set in McSorley's Old Ale House in 1860 when the pub first opened, a group of characters congregate in the bar to tell the story of the Irish in the city.

As the show pointed up, the Irish played an important role in New York from its earliest beginnings. Both Protestant and Catholic Irish favored the American Revolution, which inspired the first of many uprisings in Ireland against British rule. A chorus line of Catholics and Protestants in Colonial costume linked arms and sang a rousing march, "English Go Home."

The early Irish population of New York, the play

illustrated, consisted of merchants and professionals. But this class soon gave way to the thousands of Irish poor escaping British oppression in their homeland, including the suppression of Roman Catholicism.

Danny was too distracted thinking about Conway's murder to appreciate the play. He wondered who these people in the green Mercedes were who'd chased him. Danny remembered that Don Boyle had told him that he believed either the IRA or a Loyalist paramilitary group had threatened Finn Conway. Was it possible that these people in the car were with— who was it Boyle had mentioned—the Red Hand Brigade? Were they following Danny because they knew he was trying to find the murderer and they wanted to keep tabs on him?

It also seemed to Danny that Ian Masters might know a lot more about Conway's death than he let on. He was from Belfast. Was he mixed up with the Loyalist paramilitaries? There was something suspicious about him.

Danny decided that tomorrow after school he would go down to the offices of the *New York Voice* and read some of Conway's past columns. Maybe he would find something in the columns that would throw light on his murder.

Danny glanced at Fidelma sitting beside him, obviously enjoying herself.

"What's the matter?" Fidelma whispered. "Don't you like the show?"

Danny's attention snapped back to the stage. Sometimes it seemed Fidelma could almost read his mind. "I'm thinking about Conway."

"Don't. Just enjoy yourself."

In the early 1800s in America, anti-Irish and anti-

Catholic bigotry was widespread. Then the potato famine of 1845 in Ireland ruined the potato crops, leading to widespread death and starvation. Poor Irish Catholics began to emigrate to New York by the thousands in dark, cramped "coffin ships," originally built to transport slaves. With the stage in near darkness, the cast sang a gospel-inspired number, "Coffin Ships," that nearly brought tears to Danny's eyes.

In New York, these immigrants crowded into dirty tenements and were greeted by "No Irish Need Apply" signs when they looked for work. Despite the discrimination, they survived as bricklayers, masons, maids, and laundresses and insinuated themselves into the political process. And they did it with a sense of humor, Danny thought, as the cast launched into a tap number:

> You say we Paddys got bad tempers
> We Paddys ain't never dry
> Then you add insult to injury with:
> No Irish Need Apply.

In 1853, the Ancient Order of Hibernians was founded in New York and would from that day forward organize the St. Patrick's Day parade. By 1860, twenty-five percent of the population of New York was Irish.

In the meantime, the earlier Protestant Irish distanced themselves from these impoverished Catholics who had a reputation for drunkenness and street fighting. As the Protestant Irish assimilated into mainstream New York society, they insisted on calling themselves Scots-Irish to avoid being confused with the newcomers.

But the new Irish, with their growing numbers, their natural flair for politics, and command of the English language (although many still spoke only Irish Gaelic), had already set the stage for the Irish to dominate the political machine of New York.

The curtain fell on the stage of the Irish Repertory Theatre.

Danny and Fidelma walked into the lobby, where chilled Chardonnay and room-temperature Cabernet Sauvignon with Brie and Swiss cheese had been set out.

"You know," Fidelma said to Danny, "I never understood before tonight why Americans called themselves Irish."

"What do you mean?"

"I always thought, well, there's Irish and there's American. You're American and I'm Irish. It seemed silly to me that Americans thought of themselves as Italian and Irish and African-American." Fidelma smiled and reached for a piece of cheese. "But the Ireland most Americans have in their minds hasn't existed for over a hundred years. You know, poor, starving people in thatch cottages. We've moved way beyond that. We've one of the most booming economies in Europe right now."

"I know, the Celtic Tiger, right?" Danny said. "But the Ireland most Irish-Americans think of is the one their ancestors fled from. It's like a relic of history embedded in their minds. That history is stuck in the famine times and skips over the last one hundred years."

Fidelma laughed. "That's why when they come to Ireland they expect us all to be keeping pigs in the parlour."

"Most Irish-Americans have no first-hand knowledge of contemporary Ireland, only family stories passed down over the generations about the Ireland of their grandparents' time."

"And once a year they dress up like clowns, drink green beer, and celebrate their roots by marching in the St. Patrick's Day parade. But for the rest of the year they never give a thought at all to Ireland...the *real* Ireland."

"That's a bit harsh."

"Maybe so. But I still think it's silly that every American has a hyphenated background."

"If you stay here long enough," said Danny, "you'll be hyphenated, too."

"Never! I'll be Irish 'til the day I die."

"We'll see."

Danny spotted Matt Gill across the lobby with a wineglass in hand holding court with a group of admiring young men.

When Danny saw an opportunity, he left Fidelma talking to a set designer from Galway's Punchbag Theatre who was visiting New York, and approached Gill. "So sorry to hear about your father," Danny said, extending his hand.

Matt Gill pivoted on the toes of his shoes and faced Danny. He had handsome features: dark, deep-set eyes that sparkled with mischievous good cheer, and a strong jaw line. Thin brows arched above his eyes as if they had been plucked and penciled. He turned the corners of his mouth down pertly and ignored Danny's hand. "Oh?"

"I didn't know him, but I was there when he was shot."

"I'm touched."

Danny was taken aback by the bitter sarcasm in the young man's voice.

"He was admired by a great many people," Danny added.

"And hated by even more," Gill came back, lifting his wineglass to his lips to cover a smile.

Another young man walked up and put his arm around Matt. "Come on, let's go."

"What do you want?" Matt asked Danny, ignoring the arm around his shoulder.

"I want to find out what happened to your father."

"Why? Are you a detective?"

For a moment, Danny was at a loss for words. In the beginning, he wanted to clear Brendan—he just had to believe he was innocent. He wanted to get him out of that hellhole, Rikers Island. Now it seemed more a matter of finishing what he had started, or just the simple need to find out who and why. "The police think they have their man."

"You don't?"

"I've heard maybe GILA had something to do with it."

The guy with his arm around Matt took it off and squared up with Danny. "What about GILA?"

"Cedric's the chairman," Matt said, tossing his head toward his partner. His eyes sparkled as if he relished the idea of a fight, "and a reporter for *Out Loud!*"

Cedric Powers was well-suited to his surname. A powerfully built young man, he obviously maintained his enormous arms and chest through regular workouts. His pectoral muscles nearly burst through his tight-fitting shirt and he had the look and manner more of a longshoreman than a journalist.

"Your father tried to keep gays out of the parade," said Danny.

"Dad was a hypocrite."

"Tell me about it."

Matt Gill guffawed, spraying wine on his partner. "Who are you?"

"Just a guy from the neighborhood."

"Let's go," his partner said again.

"No, this guy amuses me. What's your name?"

"Danny...Danny O'Flaherty."

"Your family owns the funeral parlor on Two Hundred Seventh Street?" asked Matt.

"Used to. My father owned it. It was sold when he died."

"You're not an undertaker?"

"I'm a high school teacher," said Danny.

"Why are you trying to find out what happened to Dad?"

"Because a friend of mine is accused of the crime and I don't think he had anything to do with it."

Matt Gill took a sip of his wine. "Neither do I. Why would this Irish immigrant shoot my father?"

"Some people think it had something to do with Northern Ireland politics, but I don't believe it. The cops seem to think Brendan shot your father from a room in the Plaza Hotel. I don't buy that either."

"Nor do I," Gill said. "Let me give you a little piece of information. It might help."

Danny looked expectantly at the young man as he took another sip of his wine. Danny found his theatrics slightly annoying. Finally Matt said: "We were all in for quite a shock this morning when we found Dad's will."

"Really?"

"He left over twenty-five percent of a quite substantial estate to some floozy none of us ever heard of."

So, Danny thought, Old Man Conway had a girlfriend.

"And isn't it convenient for the Boyles," Matt went on, "that the mineral rights of the land they own with my parents in Ireland revert to them now? Dad was always dumb when it came to business."

"Who is the woman?"

"Like I said, nobody knew anything about her until today."

"Not even your mother?"

"Especially not my mother. She believed Dad was an old-fashioned monogamous Irish-Catholic." Gill eyed his partner and giggled. "Surprise!"

"Maybe she was just someone he wanted to help."

"*Hello?* I don't think so."

"What do you know about her?"

"Our lawyer had a private investigator do a quick check. The woman's husband was a Dominican drug dealer murdered a few years back. She's got three kids by the man. I guess she does a little hustling on the side to make ends meet." Matt laughed bitterly. "Actually, I'm delighted. I never thought the old man had it in him."

"How did the private investigator find her?"

"Easy. She's a waitress at Rory Dolan's Restaurant."

Danny felt his pulse quicken and he took a nervous sip of his wine. "What's her name?"

"Rodriguez. But she's no Latin bombshell. Her maiden name was McNamara."

Danny felt as though the floor had opened up beneath him.

Matt must have sensed something was amiss. "What's wrong? You know her?"

Just then, Fidelma walked up. "Ready to go?"

"Yes," Danny said gratefully. He held his hand out to Matt Gill. "We'll talk later."

"Yeah, right."

Danny stepped away, then stopped and turned back to Matt. "By the way," he asked, "where were *you* on St. Patrick's Day?"

Matt smiled. "We went to the demonstration in front of St. Patrick's Cathedral in the morning. Then to an anti-St. Patrick's Day party sponsored by GILA. We were protesting…" he stopped and turned to his partner, "or was it celebrating?—our exclusion from the parade."

"I see." Danny took Fidelma's arm and started to walk away, then stopped again. "Where was it?"

"Where was what?"

"The celebration?" Danny asked.

"At the Plaza."

FOURTEEN

It was Friday, March 23rd. Danny had called in to arrange for a substitute so he could visit the newspaper where Conway had worked, and have a talk with Detective Washington. He hated cutting out on school, but he had to find out what he could about whom Conway might have angered in his past columns. There just was not enough time to look into that, talk to Washington, and go to school, too.

The principal of Kennedy High School, Dr. Henrietta Zamora, had been giving Danny strange looks when he saw her in the hall. He felt under such pressure to help Brendan Grady that he'd been cutting corners on his class preparation as well. He had left early on several afternoons, skipping his final period.

Even though he felt guilty, it was nice to have a weekday away from the classroom. The weather had alternated between sun and showers. In the morning, Danny visited some of Conway's neighbors to see if they knew anything that might be useful in finding his killer. Many of Conway's neighbors remembered Danny's father.

Since Danny was the oldest son, his father had always wanted him to take over the family funeral business. But Danny never wanted any part of it. After high school, when his father pressured him to take the mortuary science course and go into business with him, Danny fled the city and enrolled in college out of state. There had always been some tension between them after that, and guilt on Danny's part for having let his father down. The eldest son in a traditional Irish family was expected to become a priest. If that was out of the question, he would at least take up the family business. Danny had done neither.

After graduating, he came back to New York and taught at Our Lady Queen of Martyrs School. But when his father died, Danny moved back into the family home above the funeral parlor. Meanwhile, the funeral business downstairs had been sold to an associate of his father, Bill Cooney, while Danny bought the apartment upstairs.

In the afternoon, after talking to Conway's neighbors, Danny headed downtown. The offices of the *New York Voice* were located in the Flatiron Building on 23rd Street overlooking Madison Square where Broadway crosses Fifth Avenue in Manhattan. The streets were clogged with pedestrians and the noise of a construction crew tearing up the sidewalk echoed between the buildings

On the way to the Flatiron Building, Danny stopped at a newsstand and bought a copy of the *New York Voice*. In the space where Fintan Conway's column usually appeared was an unsigned editorial.

MAY THE ROAD RISE UP TO MEET HIM

March 23. Fintan Conway is dead. It will be whispered in churches and bars from Far Rockaway to Yonkers. Some will say it with glee. Others with a heavy heart.

He may have been the last of the old-time Irish columnists: brash, opinionated. Some say arrogant. Reviled by his enemies; loved by his friends. A dinosaur in this information age, some called him.

A refreshingly honest old-time newspaperman, said others.

Fintan Conway, whose twice-weekly column appeared in the *New York Voice* for over twenty years, was gunned down as he marched in the St. Patrick's Day parade as grand marshal on March 17th. Heading the parade as grand marshal fulfilled a lifetime dream for Conway.

In an age of coifed talking heads, PR people disguised as journalists, and spin doctors, Conway called the shots as he saw them. Police believe that speaking his mind may have gotten him murdered.

Conway lived off controversy. He took on the privileged and the poor. He knew of what he spoke.

Born into rural poverty in County Mayo, Ireland, he rose to the heights of his career and dined with presidents. To make it in New York demands guts. Fintan Conway had guts to spare. For some, Conway was an unreformed bigot. To others he was a saint.

Love him or hate him, New York has lost an original voice. Fintan Conway is dead.

The city will never be the same.

Inside the offices of the *New York Voice,* Danny asked the receptionist for the newspaper morgue.

"Do you work for the paper?" she asked.

"No. I want to read some back issues."

The receptionist ripped a pink page from her message pad and handed it to Danny. "Just write down the date or the name of the article you're looking for. If it's fairly recent we can get it for you. There's only a nominal charge."

"I want to read Fintan Conway's columns," Danny said.

The phone rang.

"Okay. Which one? Good afternoon, *New York Voice*. Hold please." She covered the receiver with her hand. "Just write it down."

"All of them."

The receptionist looked startled. "All of them?"

"That's right."

The phone rang again. The receptionist picked it up. "*New York Voice*. Hold please." She turned back to Danny. "The most common practice is to look at these on microfiche at a library."

"I thought maybe I could read them here."

"Can't you see I'm busy?" The phone rang again. "Hold please," the receptionist said as soon as she picked it up. Then she dialed another number. "There's a gentleman down here wants to talk to you." She covered the receiver with her hand. "Name?"

"Danny O'Flaherty."

She repeated the name into the phone. "Okay, I'll send him up."

The phone rang again. "*New York Voice*. Hold please." She scribbled a floor and room number on the pink sheet and handed it to Danny. There were now four lights blinking on her console.

"Hold please," he heard the receptionist say again

as he stepped into the elevator. She called to Danny. "Ask Mr. Zhang about the columns. If he doesn't care, go ahead. Hello? Hold please."

He easily found the room number he had been given by the receptionist. Inside the office, half a dozen people worked at computer terminals in open cubicles. When he asked for Mr. Zhang, a young man pointed around his monitor, without looking away from it, to the closed door of an office.

"I came to the newspaper morgue," Danny explained to the elderly Mr. Zhang, who sat alone in a private office, "because I want to read all of Fintan Conway's columns."

"Sit down," the clerk said, shaking Danny's hand. He was a wrinkled Asian man not an inch over five feet. He wore brown Docksiders, navy blue slacks, a neatly pressed pale blue shirt, and a green bowtie. The pocket protector in the left breast pocket of his shirt held four pens and a penlight. The lenses of his horn-rimmed glasses were so thick his dark eyes swam behind them. "First of all, we no longer refer to this as the morgue. It's known as Archives and Research. You want to read all of Conway's columns?"

"All of them."

"Normally, you'd go to a library to do that."

"Yeah, but you see, I'm looking into Fintan Conway's death, and I figured you'd have all his columns in one place. It'd save me a lot of time reading them this way."

"I see. Are you with the police?"

"No."

"Private investigator?"

"You might say so," Danny hesitated. "I've been

asked by some people to see what I can find out about the murder.''

"This is a little unusual.''

"It's important. A friend of mine's life is at stake.''

Mr. Zhang got up from his desk. "Follow me.''

They took the elevator to the 8th floor. Then he led Danny down a dusty corridor. "We used to clip everything, stuff it into little brown envelopes and file it in huge file cabinets that roll electronically. They're called clip files. You push a button and alphabetical trays of clips come up.''

Mr. Zhang opened a door and turned on the light, revealing a room full of gray metal filing cabinets.

"I see.''

"Still got some of the old stuff here, but a couple years ago we started storing everything electronically. Now you go to a computer terminal, enter an electronic library, type in the names or key words, and the info appears on the screen.''

"Sounds sophisticated,'' Danny said, thinking this would be a good place to take a class on a field trip.

Mr. Zhang pointed to a single wooden desk and chair. "You can put your briefcase there.''

"Thank you.'' Danny put down his briefcase and surveyed the room.

"Conway's been around a long time. Terrible shame what happened to him. I met him on many occasions. Reporters and columnists rely on files quite a bit. I also did some research for him.'' Mr. Zhang adjusted his glasses with both hands. "He wasn't comfortable with the Internet. It all seemed like science fiction to Finn. So I did a lot of on-line research for him.''

"Like what?''

"Pulling Autotracks to check the backgrounds of people being investigated, finding missing people, looking up addresses. Things like that." Mr. Zhang fussed with a file drawer. "I wonder why anyone would want to shoot him?"

There was something insincere about the question, as if Mr. Zhang knew perfectly well why someone would want to shoot Conway. "That's what I'd like to know."

"It seems odd. Yet a man of his various opinions makes a lot of enemies, I suppose."

Danny nodded. "I guess so."

"Anyway, we have some of his columns in brown envelopes in a clip file by subject matter. We also have everything he wrote clipped and set aside in a personal file year by year. Why don't you start there."

"Okay."

"After that, I'll hook you up to the computer on the eleventh floor and you can search his name and the rest of the columns on-screen. Print them out if you want."

"I appreciate it."

Danny spent several hours reading Conway's columns, starting from 1980 when he was given his own column.

The columns constituted a virtual history of New York as seen through the eyes of an Irish-American. They explored the world of the new Irish immigrant who, unlike previous immigrants, was not cut off from the Old Country. In the days of the coffin ships, the emigrating Irish man or woman was "waked" the night before leaving for America as if he or she were dead. Once they left Ireland, in all probability, the emigrants would never be seen again.

By the 1980s, the immigrant often spent time flying back and forth to Ireland. The Auld Sod was a relatively inexpensive phone call away. Today, it was even cheaper by e-mail to "talk" to parents and loved ones back home.

Strict immigration laws in the 1980s, however, created other problems for the new Irish-Americans. Fintan Conway pulled no punches in condemning the Immigration and Naturalization Service and the Reagan Administration's immigration policies despite Reagan's teary-eyed allegiance to his "roots." Other columns addressed the influence the new Irish were having on American life and how the Irish themselves were influenced by contact with other immigrant groups from the Dominican Republic, Puerto Rico, the former Soviet Union, and Asia, not to mention home-grown Americans.

One column in particular caught Danny's eye.

THE DREAM DIES

July 14, 1995. Tito Rodriguez came to America with a dream. He wanted to own his own business in America. That dream died last week in a cramped bodega at 178th and Broadway in Washington Heights.

Rodriguez was murdered in what police say was a drug deal gone wrong. The 43-year-old native of the Dominican Republic was found dead in the back room of his tiny grocery store with two bullet wounds to the head.

Few people besides his wife and their three children will remember Tito Rodriguez. Fewer people will mourn his death. His name joins the long list of casualties in the drug wars being waged in scores of Uptown neighborhoods.

Some will say that Rodriguez—an alleged dealer of death in the form of crack cocaine— deserved to die. However, it has never been proven that he was directly involved in drug trafficking.

"My husband hated drugs," says his Irish-American wife, Kathleen. "He hated what drugs have done to this neighborhood."

Nevertheless, packages of crack cocaine were found on the murder victim's body. But that image of Tito Rodriguez as a drug dealer does not square with the man his neighbors knew.

"Tito Rodriguez was a family man and an honest businessman," says Itzak Kornblum, who owned the deli across the street from him. "There's no way he was involved in the drug business."

Did the corrupting influence of the street kill Tito Rodriguez? Did the easy money and the disregard for human life that is born of drugs poison this Dominican immigrant? It poisons many supposedly honest businessmen who indirectly benefit from the infusions of dirty cash. They know who they are.

Or is there more to this case than the NYPD is prepared to admit?

Conway went on to point a finger at various failed policies of the city, state, and federal government that seemed unable to control the problem of drugs in the city. But he reserved his harshest criticism for landlords who continued to rent to drug dealers. Managing agents and landlords had a responsibility, according to Conway, to screen prospective tenants. Landlords who rented to drug dealers should be liable for prosecution. He also called for further investigation into the death of Tito Rodriguez.

It seemed to Danny that the column showed rare compassion for an alleged drug dealer. In some of the other columns, Conway ranted against drug dealers, calling them parasites and vermin. But then, Fintan Conway's opinions were always unpredictable. Even from the first days of his column, his opinions ranged the spectrum of politics. Danny could not really find a theme that unified any of these opinions. It was as if Conway took whatever side struck him that morning as he sat down to write. And what was this veiled reference to businessmen benefiting from drugs? "They know who they are." Was that a threat or something? Did Conway leave money to Tito Rodriguez' widow just because he felt sorry for her? Or had he known something about this case that he carried to his grave?

It was almost closing time when Danny finished reading the clips. He asked Mr. Zhang if he would print out the electronic file of the clips from 1995 to the last column Conway had published on March 15th, two days before St. Patrick's Day.

It took almost an hour to print them. Danny put the columns in his briefcase and left the building. It was cold outside and the setting sun painted the glass golden on the west side of the buildings. Lights came up in the windows of the skyscrapers where workaholics hunched over their desks, struggling for closure. Second shift workers trickled up from the subways headed for their cubicles. Work never stopped in Manhattan. Even when Wall Street closed, markets in Tokyo and Hong Kong still traded, and there was money to be counted in New York. Billions of dollars in electronic assets streamed across computer screens in Manhattan every day and someone had to be there to count it no matter what time it was in New York. When the streets and sidewalks finally cleared even the rats and pigeons fought over the scraps left behind.

Danny caught a cab to the 19th Precinct station house.

FIFTEEN

THE 19TH PRECINCT station on East 67th Street in Manhattan was near the campus of Hunter College. Two imitation gaslights were set in the brick wall on either side of the station-house door and an American flag flew overhead. For a police precinct house, it looked quaint and old-fashioned with its bright red door and brick façade. About 350 uniformed NYPD personnel staffed the 19th, part of Manhattan North. The precinct, one of the most densely populated in the U.S., extended from the north side of East 59th Street to the south side of East 96th Street and from Fifth Avenue to the East River.

"Well, Mr. O'Flaherty," Detective Washington said with exaggerated enthusiasm as Danny walked into his office. "What brings you here this fine day? Have a chair."

Washington's desk looked like a smorgasbord. Cartons from two different take-out restaurants sat in front of him and it looked like the delivery boys had arrived just a few minutes before Danny. Washington pushed an antipasto salad aside and reached for one of the dozen fried shrimp he'd ordered from a Chinese place.

"Anything new?" Danny asked as he sat down.

Washington tipped back his head, let his lower jaw

open, and a deep, bellowing laugh came rumbling up from his gut. "Lots of news," he said after he'd stopped laughing. "But nothing I'm particularly inclined to share with you. A NYPD detective doesn't make a practice of discussing ongoing murder investigations with civilians. Besides, do you think I just have Conway's case to work on? I've got ten different cases on my desk right now."

"What about the people in the Mercedes?"

"Are you referring to the Calypso Green C280 Mercedes Benz?" Washington asked sarcastically as he put a fried shrimp in his mouth and chased it with a gulp of Diet 7-Up.

"Yeah. Have you found out anything about them yet?"

"We're checking into it." Washington snatched a paper coffee cup sitting in front of him and pitched it into the trashcan beside his desk, then picked up a roll and looked at it. "In the meantime, we've recovered a few spent shell casings from your buddy's room in the Plaza. Looks like he was somebody's button man."

"But have you determined from the gunshot wounds what kind of ammunition was used and whether it matches the spent shell casings?"

Muzzled by the roll in his mouth, Washington shifted his head up and down in assent. "We're looking into it," he mumbled.

"I'm sure you are."

"We still need to find the gun used to kill Conway." The detective pushed the olives in his antipasto salad aside and worked on the triangles of mozzarella.

"Have you found the person in the mask?"

"We're still trying to locate him." Washington

plucked a slice of salami from the salad. "We're working on a theory that there were two of them to make sure the job got done. Your man in the mask may have been the guy on the ground. Brendan Grady was covering him from the Plaza to make sure Conway got the bullet in case something went wrong on the street."

"Oh, give me a break. Brendan Grady didn't kill anybody."

"Crimestoppers Hotline got an anonymous phone tip just minutes before Conway was shot. Your buddy Brendan Grady's name was mentioned by the informer."

"What? I don't believe that. Who was it? What did they say?"

"You're a real piece of work, O'Flaherty." Washington thumbed an antacid tablet from a roll and put it in his mouth. "I'll bet you have a cat, don't you?"

"Yes. His name is Barnabas."

"Tell me something," Washington went on. "When you're sitting in your armchair with your cat on your lap ruminating over Fintan Conway's death, are you sipping tea?"

"Not always."

"But I'll bet you're smoking one of those curved pipes like what's his name, Sherlock Holmes."

"A meerschaum pipe? No."

"Wait, let me guess," said Washington. "You're wearing one of those funny-looking hats with a bill in the front and the back?"

When Danny didn't answer, Washington asked, "Do you carry a magnifying glass?"

"You're very amusing, Detective. Have you considered a career in stand-up comedy?"

"Listen, I do have something for you. In all your mystery stories, the victim says something on his deathbed. His dying words always mean something, right?"

"You tell me," said Danny. "You seem well acquainted with mystery stories."

"Well, I've been a cop for thirty years and I've watched lots of men die." Washington had suddenly become serious. He picked up another fried shrimp and pointed it at Danny. "They never say a damn thing that means anything."

"Okay."

"Let me tell you the kind of crap dying men say. You like stories. I'll tell you another one. One of my first cases after I made detective was on the Lower East Side. I get a call around midnight. Some scum-bucket picks up this pro skirt and—"

"Pro skirt?" Danny interrupted.

"Prostitute, O'Flaherty. Didn't they teach you anything in Catechism? Anyway, takes her to this flophouse on Bowery. I'll cut the lurid details and make it short. When he's finished with her he pumps her full of lead. Don't ask me why. To get his jollies, I guess. When I arrive at the hospital she's barely hanging on. I ask can she identify the guy. Wanna know what she says? I'll tell you. She says, 'Mama.' That's right, 'Mama.' Over and over again. Now, in one of your detective stories they'd gather the suspects in the library and announce her mother did it, right?"

"I wouldn't know, Detective."

"You want me to tell you how many people start screaming for Mama when they're on their deathbeds? Lots of 'em, that's how many."

"Interesting." Danny paused. "Speaking of dead people…you ever hear of Tito Rodriguez?"

"Sure, the Latin bandleader who died last year."

"That's Tito Puente. Tito Rodriguez was an alleged drug dealer who was killed in July, nineteen ninety-five."

"Never heard of him. Why?"

"Oh, nothing," Danny said. "He was just someone who Conway wrote about in one of his columns."

"Something special about him? Conway probably wrote about thousands of people."

"Probably so."

"Now," Washington went on, "you wanna know what Fintan Conway's last words were? The nurse told me what he said. Guess."

"Mama?"

"Guess again," said Washington.

Danny shrugged. "You seem anxious to tell me."

"Well, do you want to know?"

"Okay, I'll guess again," said Danny. "'Play it again, Sam'?"

"That's a good one. No. He said, 'Crow.'"

"Crow?"

"That's right. At first he mumbles something about Patrick—after all, he did get clocked on St. Paddy's Day. Then he says 'Crow,' and then 'Patrick' again, and then he died."

"I see," said Danny.

"So why don't you go home, put that in your pipe, and smoke it." Washington took a sip of his Diet 7-Up. He smiled and the incisor on the right side of his mouth gleamed. "Or *ruminate* on it!"

Yeah, maybe he would. Crow? Didn't Ian Masters

say something about…what was it…Black Crow Records. "Is that all, Detective Washington?"

"'Fraid so."

"Thanks for nothing."

SIXTEEN

DANNY WALKED OUT the front door of the 19th Precinct station. It was about fifty degrees and the pale afternoon sun had already given way to evening. The buildings of Hunter College crouched in gray semi-darkness and the streetlights glowed with halos of mist. When Danny stepped onto the sidewalk he felt a sudden chill.

"Spare a smoke?" asked a homeless man standing in the street.

"Sorry, no."

"Spare some change?"

Danny fished in his pocket but only had a dime in change. He put it into the man's dirty palm.

The homeless man pocketed the coin, walked away, but then turned and yelled, "Go to hell, you cheapskate!"

Danny spotted a Mercedes parked down from the station. Was it green? He pretended he didn't notice the car, turned right and walked half a block, crossed Lexington, and continued up 67th Street, keeping the blank red brick wall of the Armory to his left. If he could just catch the 6-Train to University Heights, he'd take car service from there to his apartment.

The Mercedes pulled out and swung onto 67th Street, following Danny at a distance of less than a block. It was the green Mercedes. Danny realized he had blundered. If he had turned right on Lexington, he would've been on a one-way going south. The Mercedes could not have followed him and he would have been at the 6-Train entrance in one block.

Now he turned right on Park Avenue. He stepped up his pace and the Mercedes followed. Back at Hunter College, he turned right again onto 68th Street and passed a wall with a huge, carved inscription. Danny paused to read it so he could see what the Mercedes would do:

We Are of Different Opinions at Different Hours But We Always May Be Said to Be at Heart on the Side of Truth—Ralph Waldo Emerson.

When the Mercedes stopped near him, Danny considered going back to the precinct house or stopping at a phone booth and calling Detective Washington, but the car was moving up fast to get close to him.

Danny crossed the street as if he were going into the Sylvia and Danny Kay Playhouse. When he got to the middle of the street, he glanced back and saw the Mercedes switch lanes, pick up speed again, nearly hitting a woman crossing the street with her poodle. Danny passed the theatre. At the corner of Lexington Avenue he made as if to pass the subway entrance. The Mercedes came closer. There were two men in the front seat and a third in the back. The car drew alongside as Danny stepped onto the sidewalk. He looked the other way, pretending he didn't notice the car and frantically searched for a possible means of escape.

The car pulled up beside him and came to a halt. Just as the back door of the Mercedes opened, Danny turned suddenly and leaped down the first flight of stairs into the subway station. He turned right, turned again and rushed toward the turnstile, fumbling in his pocket for his Metrocard. Then he spotted a middle-aged white man in a black turtleneck sweater racing down the subway stairs after him.

Danny dug in his other pocket for his Metrocard, found it, and swiped it through the turnstile: INSUFFICIENT FARE.

"Dammit!"

The man was halfway down the stairs. Danny threw down the card and leaped the turnstile. He hadn't skipped a fare since high school. Straight ahead was an off-hours waiting area with four round, wooden benches facing a glass partition overlooking the tracks. Danny made as if to go to the uptown train, but instead descended the stairs leading to the downtown train. He plowed through a group of high school students in baggy pants with blasting boom boxes. When he glanced back, he saw the man in the black turtleneck hesitate for a moment, then race after him. When he looked back again, the man in the turtleneck was almost on him.

"Hey, watch it!" a woman yelled at Danny. He had almost knocked her over as he plunged down the stairs. He pushed his way through more tired commuters going home from work.

When he got to the platform there was no downtown train in sight. A blind man sat on an overturned milk crate playing klezmer music on a violin. Danny ran the length of the platform and could hear his pursuer sprinting toward him. Danny's heart thumped, his chest heaving, as he glanced everywhere, looking for a way out.

"You!" the guy in the turtleneck shouted as he approached, his face flushed and beaded with sweat.

A couple standing near Danny moved away as if expecting trouble. He still looked around desperately for a way out, but faced the solid wall of the underground station. He strained to see down the track, praying a train would come.

"We need to talk," the guy said as he came within six feet. Something flashed in his hand. A knife? A gun?

Just then Danny saw the headlight of the uptown train in the tunnel across the tracks. The man was close enough to touch him now, and he reached out his right hand and pointed a gun at Danny's stomach. A Claddagh ring—two hands cradling a heart with a crown—glittered on his index finger, which rested against the trigger.

Before he had time to think about the danger, Danny leapt onto the tracks.

"Hey!"

"Oh, my God," he heard someone shout. "That guy must be crazy. He's gonna get killed!"

Danny jumped across the first set of tracks. Where's the third rail?! he wondered in a moment of panic. Hit that and he'd be electrocuted—fried by 600 volts like a piece of sausage.

"Hey, you!" someone on the uptown platform screamed. "No!"

Danny had misjudged the approach of the uptown train. It screamed out of the tunnel, banging and clattering. He glanced up and the headlight of the oncoming train blinded him.

His life did not flash before him as he had always heard it would before you died—but time did seem to slow down. The horrified faces staring down at him from the platform seemed distorted, as if he were viewing them through a Coke bottle. One image came sharply to Danny—the beautiful freckled face and lovely green eyes of Fidelma Muldoon shrouded in her halo of bright red hair on the day he had met her in the graveyard of Ballycara, Ireland. That distant morning the sun had broken through a gray mass of clouds moving in from the Atlantic and cast rays of light on the hay bales stacked in the fields. In the distance, he had seen a farmer and his helpers trying to save hay while the fine weather lasted. A flock of crows screeched from the top of an ash tree beside the road. That's when Danny noticed Fidelma peddle up on a bicycle. She was red-cheeked, with shoulder-length red hair, and she held a bunch of wildflowers.

If he lost his life he would lose her, too. Why hadn't he ever asked Fidelma to marry him?

For a moment, even the noise of the train evaporated as Danny stumbled across the final rail, flung his arms onto the subway platform, and scrambled desperately to pull himself up as the train raced toward him.

SEVENTEEN

SUDDENLY, A BURLY MAN grabbed Danny by the wrists as the train roared into the station, blasting its horn and nearly deafening him.

When the man holding his wrists yanked, Danny felt as if his shoulders were being ripped from their sockets. The man jerked him onto the subway platform, and the train knocked Danny's left shoe off as it screamed into the station.

Standing on trembling legs, Danny looked around dumbfounded, his heart hammering against his breastbone. Some people on the tracks moved away from him as if he were crazy. Danny staggered to regain his balance and looked around for his savior. But the burly man had already disappeared. His heart still pounded as he stood on the platform, disoriented. Those people in the green Mercedes had nearly gotten him killed. Who the hell were they?

"Are you okay?"

Danny turned and faced an attractive, middle-aged woman in a dark business suit and briefcase.

"You almost got yourself killed."

Danny stared at her, still in shock.

"Are you okay?" she asked again. "What in the world were you doing?"

"Someone was chasing me." Danny looked across

the tracks to see if the man in the turtleneck was still there.

"Are you sure you're not hurt?" the woman asked, already moving away from him. She stepped through the closing doors of the train.

Danny rubbed his elbow where he had banged it on the subway platform and a blade of pain stabbed his shoulder. "I'm all right," he said.

But the doors had already closed behind her and the train pulled away.

Danny had never been so close to death in his life and a million thoughts flooded his mind. He looked again across the tracks, but the man in the turtleneck was gone.

One other image besides Fidelma's had come to Danny in the moments before he was pulled onto the subway platform—the image of his father.

Danny recalled a recent conversation he had had with Fidelma over breakfast at the Metro Diner on Broadway and 100th Street. Fidelma had poured Danny and herself two cups of tea. "I never hear you mention your father," she had said.

Danny blew across the steaming tea and took a sip of the hot liquid, savoring its warmth. "What do you mean?"

"It's just that you never seem to talk about him."

"I talk about him," Danny had mumbled, putting down his teacup.

"What was he like?"

"Dad was great," Danny had answered, wondering if Fidelma believed him. "He worked hard, took care of his family, enjoyed his pint and his smokes. A devout Catholic."

"Did he ever tell you that he loved you?"

Danny had been a bit embarrassed by the question. "He made it clear every day of his life by working hard and supporting his family."

"Sure, he never paid a bit of attention to his children, so."

"What are you talking about?"

"A typical Irish father."

The waitress brought their breakfast: eggs, sausage, and another pot of tea.

"He paid attention to us!" Danny drove a fork into his sausage.

"Oh, yes, at First Communion, birthdays, Confirmation..."

Danny had brought the sausage to his mouth and chewed. His father had been a good man who kept his cards close to his chest. As a youngster, Danny had been confused about his father's job; then as a teenager, slightly embarrassed. The parents of other kids in class drove buses, worked on Wall Street; some were cops, others firemen.

Danny's father cleaned, embalmed, and buried the dead people of the neighborhood.

"I'm sure he never *told* you that he loved you."

Danny put down his fork and folded his hands under his chin. "Not in so many words, no."

"Did you ever seriously consider following in his footsteps?" Fidelma had asked, gently.

Like all little boys, there was a time when Danny wanted to grow up and be just like his father. But one day something happened that ended all that.

It was a Saturday. Danny was ten years old. He had just come back from a game of baseball with Tommy Keenan, Billy McNulty, and some of the other boys from the neighborhood. They'd been playing at the ballfield near Indian Hill Road, a five-minute walk from the O'Flahertys' apartment. That year Danny had a crush on a girl named Marie Schweitzer in his fourth grade class. She was a newcomer to the school, with dark hair and almond-colored eyes, whom Danny had befriended one afternoon as they walked home from school. He had written (and torn up) a half dozen love notes to her and had been working up the courage to share his feelings.

When Danny let himself into the apartment that afternoon thirty years ago, nobody was home.

"Mommy!"

No one answered.

Danny descended the spiral staircase in the back of the apartment that wound down into the gloom of the O'Flaherty Funeral Parlor below. Compared to the bright and often noisy apartment above, the O'Flaherty Funeral Parlor was like a vacuum where sensory texture had been—if not eliminated—then muted. Thickly insulated walls held back noises from the street and from the apartments overhead. Thick, spongy carpets padded the floors and heavy draperies kept out the sun. Carefully placed lamps emitted a gauze of lemony light. The walls were painted in sober, muted colors and a chandelier sprinkled the carpet with slivers of light. The room smelled of disinfectant and air freshener.

"Daddy?"

The lights were dimmed in the chapel. "Daddy?" There had been no funeral that day.

Danny pushed open the door of the embalming room.

His father leaned over the naked, outstretched

corpse resting on the aluminum table. The senior O'Flaherty held a needle in his hand and was stitching up an incision in Marie Schweitzer's stomach.

Danny could not have known at the time, but Marie had been hit and killed by a bus that Friday afternoon after school.

The shock of seeing his father bent over the young girl's naked, lifeless body had come as a major blow to young Danny. He fled, terrified, back upstairs to the apartment and never mentioned the incident to his father.

But from that day forward (at least through his teenage years), seeing his father eat had brought a wave of revulsion over Danny. Watching his father bring a chunk of bloody steak to his lips made Danny turn away in disgust. Later, he realized how unfair it was of him. After all, his father did what he was trained to do—and someone had to do it. But Danny could not wipe the image of the lifeless body of Marie Schweitzer from his mind.

That day he decided he would never, ever take up the same profession as his father.

"Hey, you!"

Danny looked up as the man in the turtleneck raced toward him down the uptown stairs of the subway.

Just then another uptown train roared into the station and its doors opened.

"Sixty-Eighth Street," announced the conductor. "Let the passengers off. Step in and stand clear of the closing doors."

Danny had heard the conductor's words a million times before, but never had they sounded so beautiful. As the doors opened, the sound of singing poured out of the car. A group of black men sang *a capella,* their voices booming in four-part harmony as they passed a hat: *This little light of mine, I'm gonna let it shine…*

Danny jumped into the train, moved back into another car, and found a seat as the doors closed behind him.

An overwhelming feeling of elation passed over Danny. Everything around him, the people sitting in the train, the homeless singers, the ripped movie posters on the walls, the scrawled graffiti, everything seemed bright and clear and new and promising.

As the train pulled out of the station, Danny dropped a five-dollar bill in the troubadours' hat as they passed through his car.

Looking out the window, Danny saw the man in the black turtleneck staring in at him from the platform shaking his head in disbelief.

EIGHTEEN

THE NEXT DAY, Saturday March 24th, Maureen Conway opened the door of her house with the chain still attached, in response to Danny's knock. She examined him through the slits of her pale blue eyes squinting under penciled eyebrows. Danny thought, as he watched her through the crack of the door, that her long, sharp nose and angular cheekbones gave Finn Conway's widow the look of a falcon.

"May I help you?"

"I hope so," Danny said, trying to seem as friendly and non-threatening as possible. "My name's Danny O'Flaherty. Your husband was a friend of our family."

"Yes?"

The Conways had bought their three-bedroom house on 217th Street in the Inwood section of Upper Manhattan in the late '60s. The house was in a row of six, brick two-story detached colonial-style homes. They had tiny yards that faced the towering apartment buildings of Park Terrace Gardens. These six suburban-looking homes surrounded by urban Manhattan had been built by a man who lived in one and rented the rest. In the upwardly spiraling real-estate market of today's Manhattan, the houses were worth a small fortune.

"I'm so sorry about your husband," Danny said.

"How can I help you?"

"I'm trying to find out what happened."

Maureen Conway's eyes narrowed and she left the chain on the door.

"The man they arrested is a friend of mine," Danny explained. "I believe he's innocent."

"My husband was gunned down in the street," she said in a shrill voice, "and you're worried about the man who murdered him? Get out. Get out of here."

"I want to find out who *really* did it," Danny said. "I want the person who killed your husband to pay." Danny couldn't help thinking that if she knew about her husband's mistress, Maureen Conway herself might have had a good motive to murder her husband. Obviously, she didn't pull the trigger, but she may have hired someone to do it. "I want to find the murderer."

The lines around Maureen Conway's eyes softened and the corners of her mouth curled upward in a forced smile as she undid the chain on the door. She wore a bright blue jogging suit and sneakers and appeared to have been exercising.

Mrs. Conway led Danny to a wicker sofa where he sat down. The house was furnished with new, modern furniture. Plaques, awards, clippings, and family photos of the Conway girls filled the walls of the living room. Conspicuously absent were images of their son—Matt Gill.

A mahogany gun case with glass doors stood against one wall (an unusual piece of furniture for Manhattan) and five high-powered rifles with scopes rested in the case.

With weights in hand, Mrs. Conway climbed back

aboard the treadmill she had obviously been walking on when Danny had knocked.

She has nine children, Danny thought, and she's alone at a time like this? Odd. "Was your husband a hunter?" Danny asked, nodding toward the gun case.

"My husband was a strong believer in the Second Amendment to the U.S. Constitution," she answered as she began walking at a fast clip on the treadmill.

Again Danny was struck by the contradictory nature of Conway's views. It was rare to meet anyone vehemently opposed to the death penalty who had an interest in guns, much less someone who also supported abortion rights while at the same time condemning homosexuality. It was quite a mixed bag of beliefs.

"He did hunt as a child," she added. "He was raised in the country, you know. On a farm in County Mayo at the foot of Croagh Patrick. In fact, we still own land there. We bought sixty acres together with the Boyles' years ago."

"The holy mountain?" Matt had mentioned that. "Don Boyle?" Boyle had also said something about the two having property in Ireland.

"Yes. Finn's dream was to retire to that property. I was never much interested but I would have done it…to please him."

"I got the impression your husband and Don Boyle had…differences, but they used to be friends."

"We all used to be great friends, Don and his wife, and Finn and I. But the men couldn't get along, which is a shame. I still think the world of Diane Boyle. She and Don sent a beautiful wreath. You want a cup of coffee?" Mrs. Conway asked. "I have a warm pot in the kitchen. Help yourself."

"No thanks."

Mrs. Conway increased the speed on the treadmill and grit her teeth as she walked/jogged. Danny got up from the sofa and walked over to have a better look at the guns. There were three Brownings and two Mossbergs. Danny noticed an empty space in the rack of guns. "Tell me, Maureen, is a gun missing from the case?"

"Call me Mo." Sweat had broken out on her forehead and she grimaced from the exercise. "My son, Matt, borrowed a gun to loan to an actor friend who needed a prop for a play."

"When was that?"

"About a week and a half ago," she said, huffing.

Just before St. Patrick's Day, Danny thought. "What kind of gun was it?"

"Oh, I don't know. I hardly notice the difference between one car and another, much less guns," she said between clenched teeth, sweat glistening on her forehead. "Why?"

"Oh, nothing." Danny paused a moment. "Who did he loan it to?"

"Friend of his. Cedric Powers."

Aha, thought Danny. "I don't see any pictures of Matt. I understand he's a fine dancer. You must be proud of him."

"I am proud of him," Mo said as she got off the treadmill. She put down the weights, stood in the center of the room with legs slightly apart, her right fist balled and held straight out in front of her, her left arm bent at her side. "But unfortunately, my husband did not share my opinion." She lunged forward, throwing her left foot out, nearly kicking Danny in the face.

Danny ducked, fell backwards, and skootched farther back in the sofa.

"Finn strongly disapproved of our son's lifestyle."

"I see," Danny said, as if it were news to him. He wondered why Mo hadn't gone to the theatre the other night since her husband had been honored, and Matt had been asked to speak.

"He even wanted to cut Matt out of the will." Mo followed through with her right fist, thrusting it within inches of Danny's nose.

"But he died before he had the chance," Danny mused. "And your husband made sure GILA didn't get into the parade, and Cedric Powers..."

Mrs. Conway glanced at the gun case, then back at Danny. "What are you suggesting, Mr. O'Flaherty?" She relaxed her martial arts stance and started doing knee bends.

"Nothing, nothing. My girlfriend and I went to the performance of Fran McCormick's play last night."

"Oh, him. The way he's airing all the dirty laundry of the Irish is disgraceful. He's such a publicity hog."

Danny fought the urge to say, *Like your husband?* "Your son gave a very moving speech," he lied.

"Matt's good at that sort of thing—just like his father. It's a shame the two never saw eye-to-eye. Despite all their differences they were so much alike." Mrs. Conway collapsed in a recliner across the room, lifted her legs toward the ceiling, and started pedaling an imaginary bicycle in the air.

Mo Conway didn't seem to be in much grief, Danny observed. But everyone deals with death in a different way.

When she stopped pedaling and fell back in the

chair, for a moment Danny thought she was going to cry. Her eyes gleamed with moisture and she seemed to be holding herself in check. Or was she putting on a good show?

Danny waited a moment then changed tack, "Matt mentioned a woman…"

Maureen Conway sat up and gave a strangled moan like a wounded animal. "That hussy!" she shrieked. "I could kill her."

Danny waited while she collected herself. "Did you know about her before the reading of the will?" Danny asked.

"I suspected something," she whispered. "A woman always knows."

"Do you think she may have had something to do with your husband's death?"

"It's entirely possible," Mo said without hesitation. "After all, she inherited quite a lot of money."

"Will you contest it?"

She shrugged. "Of course not. If Finn wanted her to have it, then she should. Those were his wishes. Just like the living will."

"The what?"

"Finn didn't want his life extended unnecessarily. He signed a living will. He wanted to be removed from any life-prolonging devices if he was ever in a situation where the hope of recovery was remote."

That surprised Danny. He knew from reading the columns that Conway had been opposed to euthanasia and even removing patients from respirators. "Was he taken off life support?"

"Yes," Mrs. Conway whispered. "Yes, he was."

NINETEEN

DANNY SAT AT his desk in his apartment after coming home from Conway's house, and with barely controlled excitement, opened the manila envelope that had just been delivered. His aunt had come through— Danny had a copy of the autopsy on Fintan Conway.

M.E. Case No: L31-6493
Compartment No: 01559

OFFICE OF CHIEF MEDICAL EXAMINER
CITY OF NEW YORK

AUTOPSY
State of New York
City and County of New York
Borough of Manhattan

Age: 63
Approximate Weight: 250 lbs.
Height: 6'2''

AUTOPSY PERFORMED BY Dr. Miriam Meyrowitz, Associate Medical Examiner on March 21, 2001. In the presence of Drs. Rivera, Connor, and Polaski.

I hereby certify that I, Miriam Meyrowitz, M.D., have performed an autopsy on the body of Fintan Patrick Conway at Manhattan Mortuary on the 21st day of March, 2001, two hours after the death. Said autopsy revealed:

External Examination:
The body is that of a 6' 2'', 250 lbs. white male appearing the stated age of 63 years. Rigor mortis is complete throughout the body with dorsal fixed lividity. Scalp hair is medium length, straight, gray. No facial hair. Irises are blue; the eyes in mid-position. External auditory canals, nares and oral cavity are free of foreign material and abnormal secretions. Nasal skeleton intact. Dentation normal, with some deterioration from poor maintenance. Head, neck, chest, abdomen, back, extremeties and anus are unremarkable (except as described below). Old scars on right quadrant from prior excision of appendix.

Evidence of Recent Injury:
What follows is a description of gunshot wounds. Note, order of description does not presume the order in which they were inflicted upon decedent.

Gunshot Wound 1 of Chest:
A gunshot wound of entrance is located over the left anterior chest at a point 18'' below the top of the head and 6'' left of the posterior axillary midline. The entry defect is 3/8'' in diameter with 1/8'' rim of abrasion. The wound perforates the 6th left posterior lateral rib, thoracic aorta, right upper lobe of lung, lodging in chest 12'' below top of the head and 7 1/8'' right of the anterior midline. A small caliber, non-jacketed,

lead missile is recovered, labeled, and placed in evidence envelope.

Gunshot Wound 2 of Trunk:
A gunshot wound of entrance is located over the anterior aspect of trunk, 26" below the top of the head and 2" right of the posterior midline. Entry wound is ³/₄" in diameter. Missile perforates the 8th and 9th right posterior ribs, right lower lobe of the lung and exits anterior chest wall at 12" below top of the head and 3" right of the midline in a trajectory of right to left, upward and frontward.

Gunshot Wound 3 of Right Shoulder:
A gunshot wound of entrance is located on right anterior shoulder where right clavicle joins shoulder blade. Entry wound is ³/₄" in diameter. Missile causes extensive damage to shoulder blade, clavicle, and is deflected off into breastbone. A small caliber, non-jacketed led missile is recovered, labeled, and placed in evidence envelope.

Internal Examination:
Organ Weights:
Heart, 340 grams; lungs, right—410 grams, left—380 grams; liver, 1800 grams; spleen, 95 grams; kidneys, 130 grams each; brain, 1350 grams.

Cause of Death:
Gunshot wounds (3) to chest, abdomen, shoulder. Homicide.

TWENTY

DANNY LOOKED UP from the autopsy report. Anus unremarkable? He stroked Barnabas, who lay sleeping on his lap, gently purring with pleasure as if he were having a pleasant dream. "Is that all a man's life amounts to?" Danny asked his cat. "How much your heart weighs? Never mind the affairs of the heart, the heartache, the heartbreak, the heartfelt joy of life—you're telling me all that matters in the end is that your heart weighs three hundred forty grams and your butt is unremarkable?"

The cat said nothing.

That was his aunt's world of the coroner's office, and Detective Washington's. "You know, Aunt Bertie always seems like such a happy-go-lucky person," Danny went on. "How odd that her work is so morbid. Maybe being close to death every day makes her carefree, knowing that we'll all end up in the same place. Our lives can be reduced to statistics as dull as the weight of our organs. Might as well enjoy life while you can, right Barney?"

Barnabas did not appear to be listening.

Whatever his aunt thought, Danny was grateful she'd delivered on the autopsy report. But he still believed a person's story—even the story of his death—amounted to more than a catalog of body parts. Now he tried to see if the report cast any light at all on who killed Finn Conway. *It's about forensics,* he could hear Detective Washington say, *forensics.*

As Danny read through the report again he kept thinking that Fintan Conway may not have been a saint, but he deserved better than to be chopped up on an aluminum autopsy table and parceled out like items in a butcher shop. Danny had never thought of it before, but suddenly he realized how invasive murder truly was. A death by natural causes evoked sadness among the survivors, then the deceased was buried with ceremony and tears. But murder summoned horror and pity, then curiosity and a macabre celebrity. The victim no longer belonged to the family, but became public property. His things were picked through in a search for clues. His whereabouts documented. Then, the final indignity: his body opened and examined, his organs cataloged and weighed.

Danny stroked Barnabas' head as he purred, curled up in his lap. He glanced back at the autopsy report looking for anything that might give him some idea of how to get on with finding Conway's killer.

A couple of things stuck out as he read the report once again. First, the upward trajectory of the bullet to the trunk did not suggest that the shots were fired from above—certainly not from the 9th floor of the Plaza Hotel. If the shots didn't come from the Plaza then Brendan was clear.

The second thing that caught Danny's attention was that the bullets recovered from the body were small caliber. Again, you couldn't fire a small-caliber gun all the way from the 9th floor of the Plaza and kill somebody on Fifth Avenue. Impossible. Besides, the abrasions mentioned in the report further suggested that Conway had been shot at close range. All this seemed obvious—even to an amateur. Had Washington intentionally misled the press with the Plaza Hotel theory? Nobody shot Fintan Conway from the Plaza. Danny knew that. So did Washington.

But why didn't Brendan want any help? He might serve life in prison if he was convicted. What was Brendan trying to hide? And there was something—actually a lot—about this Ian Masters that bothered Danny. More importantly, who were these people following him in the green Mercedes who'd nearly killed him twice? If it hadn't been for that man who pulled him onto the platform, he'd be laid out downstairs right now at the O'Flaherty Funeral Parlor, and tomorrow he'd be pushing up daisies.

Danny had first thought he'd report the incident in the subway to Washington but he decided against it. The next time he saw him, he wanted something substantial to offer in Conway's murder. He didn't want to go to Detective Washington as the *victim* of a crime. But now he was fuming. Surely Washington had seen this report. How stupid did he think Danny was? It was obvious Fintan Conway was not shot from above. That removed suspicion from Brendan. What was Washington trying to cover up? Danny took the detective's card from his wallet and reached for the phone. He felt like giving him a piece of his mind.

But he didn't call him. He wanted to follow up instead on the information Washington had given him about Conway's last words. Danny picked up the phone on the oak, clawfoot end table beside his recliner, dialed information, and asked for the number of Black Crow Records.

"Black Crow," a man answered.

"My name is Roger Devins," Danny began, "and I own a bar in Queens."

"So what?"

"I'm trying to book some bands and I'm wondering if you can tell me how to get in touch with Dead Leper Cons."

"With what?"

"You've heard of Ian Masters?"

"Oh, him. Look, buddy, this ain't no booking agency."

"I understand Ian has a recording contract with you."

The guy on the other end of the line snorted. "Yeah, Masters rented studio time. He plans to do an album. Wouldn't call it a recording contract, exactly."

"How much does something like that cost?"

"Something like what?"

"Enough studio time to record an album?"

"It varies. What kind of music? What kind of instruments? Listen, who are you, anyway?"

"I know another band that wants to record an album. I thought maybe you'd be interested."

"Maybe I am."

"How much would it cost to record an album?"

"Like I said, it all depends. Figure fifty bucks an hour for the sessions, including the engineer. A bigger studio than mine might cost three or four times that much. So, that's a low price to start with. Then it all depends on how prepared you are. You got solid arrangements and you're all rehearsed and ready, figure a couple hours per song."

"Okay, say this band wants to do a dozen songs,"

Danny said, calculating. "Two hours per song times fifty dollars. That's twelve-hundred bucks."

"You ain't listening to me. Time is money. You come in and screw around like a lot of deadbeat musicians with sudden money do, it's gonna cost. You try to come up with ideas in the studio, show up drunk, whatever, you can multiply that by twenty and not be out of bounds."

"I see. You think Masters is a deadbeat?"

"No, I think Masters is a dork brain. There's a difference."

Danny decided not to pursue the subtleties of the distinction. "I see."

"At some point the engineer might just get fed up with the whole shooting match, fire your band as a client, and walk."

"Let's suppose that doesn't happen," Danny said. "And they finish the album."

"Okay. They finish it. They come out of here with either a DAT tape, which costs about twenty bucks, or a single master CD. You take that to a CD pressing company and get a thousand CDs made for a thousand bucks, including the boxes, some one- or two-color inserts, shrink-wrapping..."

Danny scribbled notes in the margins of the autopsy report.

"Your band can sell them out of the back of their van, or at gigs, or whatever and that's the end of their expense. If you want to sell them in stores you need a UPC barcode and probably a distributor. Then there's promotion—"

"I get the idea. What about Ian Masters? How much you think his session will cost him?"

"If he's sober and has his crap together, he can get

out of here for five thousand dollars with a dozen
songs and a DAT. That's what he's thinking, anyway.
He put the five thousand cash up front.''

"When?"

"He starts recording next week." The guy gave a
short laugh. "Solo album. Ian Masters unplugged—"

"No, I mean when did he pay you?"

Danny could hear papers being shuffled. "The seventeenth.''

"St. Patrick's Day?"

"I guess so. Hey, what is this? Are you a cop or
something?''

Danny hung up.

"Ian Masters had five grand cash on St. Patrick's
Day," Danny said to Barnabas.

Barnabas stood in Danny's lap, arched his back,
and yawned.

"What did he do, win the Publishers Clearing
House Sweepstakes?" It was hard to imagine Masters
screaming "Oh, my God!" as Ed McMahon handed
him a check the size of a billboard. As Danny mulled
this over, the telephone rang. It was Fidelma. She was
supposed to come over.

"Sorry I'm late," said Fidelma. "Have you found
out anything about Fintan Conway?"

"Yes. Brendan could not possibly have shot Conway from the Plaza."

"I knew it!"

"And somebody is trying to kill me."

"Good Lord, who?"

"Those same guys in the green Mercedes who followed us from Rikers Island. They chased me down
into the subway and I nearly got run over by a train."

"Danny, no! Are you all right?" Fidelma's voice

trembled. "I couldn't bear it if anything happened to you. You must be careful."

"I'm okay."

"What do they want?"

"I don't know. I think they know I've been asking questions. Someone doesn't want me to find out who *really* killed Conway."

"Oh, Danny. When I asked you to help, I never dreamed it would lead to something like this. Promise me you'll be careful, love."

"Don't worry," Danny said, but he loved it when Fidelma worried about him. "You know, when I was facing death down in the subway…"

"Yes?"

Danny wasn't sure what he wanted to say. "Well, it makes you realize what's important in life."

"I'm sure it does."

"It made me realize how important you are to me."

"Danny, you're all the world to me. You know I love you, but I'm so worried. Why won't Brendan let us help him?" Fidelma asked. "I knew he was stubborn, but he could die in there. What makes you say he couldn't have possibly done it?"

"I just read the autopsy report. Conway was shot at close range by a small-caliber handgun, most likely."

"The masked man?"

"Maybe so. One thing's clear, he wasn't shot from the Plaza. But Brendan's still covering for something and we have to find out what." Danny could hear the subway banging in the background and the noise of the train's horn coming over the phone. "When are you going to be here?"

"I'm getting on the train now. I'll be there in twenty minutes."

"Good, I'll take you out to dinner. We'll go over to that Italian place—Roberto's—in the Bronx. Okay?"

"Grand."

Danny hung up and paced the room while he waited for Fidelma. If Ian Masters had five thousand dollars on St. Patrick's Day, was it possible someone paid him to shoot the grand marshal? But why? Besides, would anybody gun down a man for five thousand bucks? Ask Washington, Danny thought. He probably knew the going rate for a hit in Manhattan.

Danny continued pacing, and when a half hour had passed and Fidelma had still not shown up, he went to the kitchen to make tea. He used to hate tea, but after drinking gallons of it in Ireland when he lived there for a year, he had finally acquired a taste for it.

As the water boiled, Danny moved aside the curtain in the kitchen. The green Mercedes was parked in front of the deli across the street. But there was no one in it. I ought to call the cops, thought Danny.

Just then the teakettle whistled and Danny heard the door buzzer go off. He switched off the heat under the kettle, dropped four teabags into the Belleek teapot he had bought in Dublin, and poured in the boiling water. "Coming."

Odd that Fidelma didn't ring from downstairs.

When Danny opened the door, two men in black ski masks stood behind Fidelma. One held Fidelma's arm twisted behind her back.

The other held a gun to her head.

TWENTY-ONE

THE MEN IN THE black ski masks shoved Fidelma in front of them and rammed their way into the apartment.

"What the hell?" Danny said as they knocked him back against the end table.

"Don't argue," Fidelma whispered, her face twisted into a grimace.

The tall one threw Fidelma on the recliner, and Barnabas skittered off into a bedroom.

Thanks, Barney.

The short one kept the gun to Fidelma's head.

"No heroics, Cowboy," the tall one said to Danny. He had a thick Irish brogue and a rough voice that one was not inclined to argue with. "We're not going to hurt you. We just want to talk."

"You break into my apartment and hold a gun to my girlfriend's head because you want to *talk?*"

Fidelma glanced at Danny with frightened eyes as if to say, *don't say any more, please.*

"We mean you no harm," the short one said, holstering the gun. Although dressed in the same bulky clothes and ski mask as the tall one, Danny realized when she spoke that the shorter of the two was a woman.

The tall one pushed Danny into a chair.

"You're the ones in the green Mercedes," Danny said. "I saw the car parked downstairs. What do you want? Why have you been following me? Who are you?"

"We're with ARM."

"What's that?"

"Army of the Republican Movement," Fidelma whispered. "A splinter of the IRA."

"The IRA sold out the movement with this peace agreement. We've had nothing to do with them since then."

"The Good Friday Agreement?"

"That's right."

"Now I get it," Danny said. "Conway wrote columns in favor of the Good Friday Agreement. He supported decommissioning and urged all the paramilitaries to lay down their arms. He called the IRA murderers and thugs. So you killed him?"

"You don't know what you're talking about," the tall one replied. "We tried to *stop* Conway's death."

"You what?"

"We were trying to stop Conway's murder."

"Then you did know he was going to be shot?"

"We knew it was being planned by a group sympathetic to the Red Hand Brigade."

Danny had heard of the Red Hand Commandos, a loyalist paramilitary organization, and he had heard of the Red Hand Defenders, another Protestant extremist group that was also opposed to the Good Friday Agreement. According to a recent article in the *Irish Echo,* both the Red Hand Defenders and a group called The Orange Volunteers had been added to the U.S. State Department's list of terrorist organizations. Making the list meant that the groups' assets were frozen, members were ineligible for U.S. visas, and financial support to the groups was against the law. And Boyle had told Danny something about the Red Hand Brigade at the pub.

"Why would the Red Hand murder Conway?" Fidelma asked skeptically. "He was no threat to them."

"Exactly. It was a set-up. We thought they planned to kill Conway and blame it on ARM. Make us look bad, and turn our Irish-American support against us. We got wind of the plot. Your friend Brendan has been with us for over ten years. He's a field commander. Very experienced. We sent him in to the Plaza to try to stop Conway's murder."

So Brendan *had* been telling the truth all these years about his involvement in the Irish troubles!

"What happened?"

"We got triple-crossed. The whole plot to hit Conway was a hoax. They had no intention of killing him. The Red Hand Brigade lured us into the Plaza Hotel by putting out false information and leaving a lot of phony evidence in the room. Spent shell casings, for example. Brendan went to the hotel room but there was no one there. We think it was just a diversionary tactic to keep us busy trying to defuse a situation that didn't even exist. Maybe they figured they'd let the cops take one of ours. I'll bet they were surprised that someone else actually did shoot Conway, anyway. It worked perfectly for them. Now they can blame it on Brendan."

"And Brendan can't defend himself," Danny said bitterly, "or else he'll reveal all your plans and your identities."

"I'm going to trust you," the tall man said.

Danny noticed a Claddagh ring on his index finger.

"I'm asking you to trust us." The man reached up and pulled the ski mask off his face. It was the same guy who'd almost gotten him killed in the subway.

"Why should we trust you?" Danny asked. "You followed me from school. Followed us from Rikers Island. Nearly got me killed in the subway."

"If Brendan talks," the man said, ignoring Danny's rant, "he may prove he had nothing to do with Conway's death. But he'll incriminate himself. After all, he's an officer of ARM. He'll still spend time behind bars."

"You mean incriminate *you*," Danny said.

"We've got to help him," Fidelma put in.

"If you want to help him, leave it to us." The man said, dipping his head toward his partner. "Brendan had nothing to do with Conway's murder—on the contrary, he tried to stop the shooting. But he's not likely to be believed."

"What will you do?"

"Just leave it to us."

"Why have you been following me?" Danny asked. "You nearly killed me."

"You nearly killed yourself in the subway. That wasn't our fault. At first we thought you might be with the Red Hand Brigade, trying to get to Brendan, maybe to kill him. We had to follow you to see what you were up to. One of our informers saw you talking to the cops after the shooting. Then we realized you were actually trying to help your friend. Brendan told us he wanted you two kept out of it. All we wanted to do was talk, but you kept running. When we stopped your girlfriend downstairs and told her we needed to talk to you, she resisted. We had to come in here this way. But we just wanted to find you and tell you that the best way to help Brendan is to stay out of the way.''

"But what about Conway?" Danny asked.

"What about him?"

"What happened? Who *did* kill him?"

"We don't know. But we do know it had nothing to do with us or the Red Hand Brigade. We have moles inside their organization. They had nothing to do with it, but we don't care if they do get blamed for it. To be honest, we don't think it had to do with Irish politics at all."

"Then who shot him?"

The short one looked at Danny, then Fidelma, then back to Danny. "You find out," she said.

TWENTY-TWO

AFTER THE TWO MEMBERS of ARM left the apartment, Danny held Fidelma for hours as she trembled in his arms, badly shaken. She stayed the night with Danny—a rare occasion—and they made love almost fiercely, a reaffirmation that they were both alive. Later, they fell asleep in each other's arms. Fidelma cried out several times during the night, reliving the frightening assault.

They spent all of Sunday together, never leaving the apartment. Danny and Fidelma argued about whether they should tell Detective Washington about the attack by ARM. Fidelma thought they should. That surprised Danny, since Fidelma had overstayed her visa and was illegally in the country. Even though he had made some progress toward getting Fidelma permanent resident status, he knew she didn't want to bring her precarious situation to the attention of the immigration authorities. But she was more worried about Brendan than herself. And she was outraged by the attack.

Danny argued that they should keep it to themselves and see if ARM in fact did help Brendan. Still, Fidelma was upset and nervous.

On Monday, March 26th, Danny called school to say he could not get there until later. He would need coverage for his first couple classes. Then Danny drove Fidelma to her own apartment and stayed with her for a while. But he had to get to class. Finally, he left her, but did not get to school until after noon.

Five minutes before Danny's last-period class was to end, the door opened and the principal of John F. Kennedy High School, Dr. Zamora, walked in and took a seat in the rear of the classroom. Danny planned to go to Rory Dolan's Restaurant immediately after school to speak with Kate Rodriguez. The last thing he needed was a talk with the principal.

However, Danny was not surprised by the principal's visit. He had taken a personal day on Friday in order to go to the *New York Voice* and talk to Detective Washington at the 19th Precinct. Since the shooting on St. Patrick's Day, he had used up all his personal days running around looking into the murder. Then he had missed all his classes this morning because Fidelma wanted him to stay with her.

The principal, Dr. Henrietta Zamora, wore a well-pressed navy wool jacket with matching pants, and a white silk blouse buttoned to the top. A diskette in one hand and a yellow legal pad in the other, she eyed Danny through a pair of stylish, horn-rimmed glasses. Her short black hair was neatly arranged and her lips lightly touched with rose-colored lipstick. Still, she had the demeanor of a no-nonsense bond trader on Wall Street.

When Danny dismissed the class, Dr. Zamora stood up and approached his desk as he stuffed books and papers into his briefcase and planned his escape.

"Henrietta." He checked his watch, anxious to get out. "What a nice surprise."

Dr. Zamora had taken over the year before from a

frumpy older gentleman who had followed a strict policy of *laissez faire* in the many years of his tenure as principal. With some pressure from the school board, he had finally retired in order to dedicate more time to his baseball card collection and had decided to branch out into professional bowling memorabilia.

"Everything okay?" asked Dr. Zamora.

"Just fine."

"You want to talk about Friday?"

Danny hesitated a moment.

Dr. Zamora quickly filled the gap. "And where were you this morning? I didn't even have time to get a substitute. Mrs. Zeman had to cover your classes."

"I've got a lot on my plate right now," said Danny.

Henrietta Zamora, born in Puerto Rico and raised in New York, had a doctorate in education from Baruch College and possessed the single-minded drive and spirit of a reformer. "I'm not running a home for troubled teachers here." Henrietta pulled one of the students' chairs up to his desk. "We need to talk."

"Frankly, I don't have a lot of time right now," said Danny, glancing again at his watch.

Dr. Zamora looked at the Roman numerals on her own Cartier, and sat down.

A neat stack of essay tests sat in the upper right hand corner of the desk with a small glass globe holding them down. In the upper left, the Social Studies text lay open to the section on the civil rights movement. The only other thing, a one-page typed agenda for the day's activities, sat directly in the center of the desk with a black Flair pen atop it.

"I see you are well organized for class."

"I have to be."

"Especially when you miss half the day."

Danny drummed his fingers on his desk.

"I'll get to the point," Dr. Zamora said as she settled herself in her chair. "I'm concerned about you. You missed school on Friday. Are you sick?"

"Not exactly."

"Mind telling me exactly what *is* going on?"

"Like I said, I have a lot on my plate right now."

"Oh, great. That explains everything. You don't think the rest of us have busy lives?"

"I'm sure you do. Look, Henrietta. I get ten sick days per year. Three of those can be used as personal days. You worked under the contract. You know what I'm entitled to."

Mention of the contract seemed to quiet the principal. Then she said, "All of my teachers are busy. Mrs. Zeman is in an Off-Broadway show. Mrs. Andriani is an adjunct instructor in the evening at City College."

"Really?" Danny stood with his briefcase in his hand. He was anxious to see Kate, not just to talk about Joey, but to find out more about her relationship with Fintan Conway. Why had Conway mentioned her in his will? And for such a large amount.

"You're a damn good teacher, Danny. Probably one of the best I've got here. We both know that." Dr. Zamora turned the palm of her hand over and examined her lifeline. "You're not looking for another job, are you?"

Danny laughed, set his briefcase down, and pulled up a chair. "You know of any?"

"Of course not. How is Joey Rodriguez doing?"

"Needs to focus." Danny sat down. "He's a bright kid who has gotten in with a very rough crowd."

"Yes, he has." She paused a moment. "How long have you been teaching now, Danny?"

Danny thought he caught a note of condescension in her voice. Was she going to give him another one of her lectures about the "real world"?

"Almost fifteen years."

Dr. Zamora reached down and pulled a pocket calendar from her purse. "I'm planning a special faculty meeting on curriculum for next week. Can I count on you to give a presentation on how to enrich the Irish Famine curriculum? Maybe the story of Irish immigration in the History and Social Studies programs?"

"No problem." Danny rummaged in his briefcase looking for his own appointment calendar. What was it she really wanted? he wondered, anxious to get out of there.

Dr. Zamora penciled in something on her calendar and looked up. "I also understand you're involved with the police in some way."

"What?" Danny was surprised that word had gotten as far as the principal.

She examined him curiously and placed her pen carefully on the desk. "I hope it's not interfering with your teaching."

"Well, I do have a life outside of this classroom."

"Indeed you do." She picked up her pen again and looked at it as if she had never seen it before.

"I give these kids one hundred percent while I'm here," Danny said, annoyed. "I thought you knew that."

"I used to know that." Dr. Zamora put the pen down in the exact center of the desk, leaned back in her chair, and folded her hands as if in prayer. "What's this business with the police all about?"

"I'm not sure I know what you're referring to."

Dr. Zamora stood up. "Okay, Danny, play it your way. I'll find out what you're up to. You seem to forget I was once an instructor at the John Jay College of Criminal Justice."

"I didn't know that."

"Oh, yes. I hope you're not getting in over your head."

"Now wait a minute, Henrietta. I'm a teacher. I give one hundred percent to these kids in the classroom."

"You said that already. But playing detective is not exactly your role here."

Danny stared at her, stunned. So, she *already* knew what he was up to.

"Do you have a problem with our school?" she asked.

"I told you, no. You know me. I tell the truth. If I don't like something about the school, I say so. And I'm telling you. Everything is fine."

"If you weren't so high-minded, maybe you wouldn't still be here."

"I like it here."

"Do you really?"

"Listen, Henrietta, I'm meeting someone after class. The mother of one of my students, actually. To talk about his work."

"Which student?"

"Joey Rodriguez." Danny snapped his briefcase shut.

"I think you've probably misjudged Joey."

"What do you mean by that?"

"I grew up surrounded by kids like him. It's good of you to take an interest. But I wouldn't waste a lot of time on him."

Danny turned to the principal, stung by the remark. "What the hell is that supposed to mean, Henrietta?"

"You've got other kids who need your attention. Joey Rodriguez will probably end up in Sing Sing—"

"I can't believe you can sit there and—"

"Look, you know we have files that only principals and vice-principals see."

"What are you telling me?"

"Hold on, Danny, hold on. Do it your way. I'm just warning you. You have a responsibility to *all* the kids in your classroom."

"Don't you worry. I know my responsibilities."

"I hope you do," said Dr. Zamora. "However, let me remind you of a responsibility you may have overlooked." She reached into her bag again. "I'm quoting from Administrative Memorandum Number Nine. 'All teachers should prepare three sets of absentee lesson plans for each subject taught. These plans should be substantive in nature. It is imperative that there is teacher follow-up… Students must recognize that their education does not stop because the teacher is absent on a given day… Teachers should have specific instructions for the substitute…'"

"All right, all right."

Dr. Zamora smiled as if pleased she had made her point. "Now, tell me about this investigation you're involved in."

"Really, Henrietta. What I do off school grounds is my business."

"Of course it is. But I want to make sure it doesn't interfere with your work here."

"What are you getting at? Have you had any complaints about my work?"

"Not exactly. But I did get an unusual call this morning, from a Detective Washington."

"You what? What did he want?"

"He had a few questions about you."

"About me? What kind of questions?"

"Nothing much. Don't worry, I gave you a good character reference."

Character reference? Danny picked up his briefcase and stood, fuming. "See you tomorrow," he said.

Dr. Zamora smiled for the second time since she'd arrived. "I hope so." Then, in a rare display of vulnerability, added, "You know, in a way I admire the faith you have in these kids. You never turned cynical after all these years in the classroom."

"Is that all, Henrietta?"

"One more thing."

Danny clutched his briefcase. "I've got to go."

"I hope you know what you're doing," she said. "You know, you are really approaching a situation of excessive absenteeism. You know as well as I do that this could lead to disciplinary hearings. Miss any more classes without a valid excuse and I'll write you up."

"Is that all?"

"Be careful, Danny."

TWENTY-THREE

R<small>ORY</small> D<small>OLAN'S</small> Restaurant & Bar on McLean Avenue in Yonkers, with its live Irish music, private party room, and seating for 400, was a well-known gathering spot for Irish-Americans in New York, and also where Kate Rodriguez worked.

The hostess greeted Danny with a smile. "Good evening."

Danny was certain now that neither the Red Hand nor ARM had anything to do with the death of Fintan Conway. That salved Danny's conscience that he might be withholding evidence from the police by not telling them about the Red Hand or ARM. Clearly no one could have shot Conway from above in the Plaza, meaning that the killer *had* to be at street level. Which left the masked gunman, or woman. Gunperson? But how do you find a person in a mask? He was also still wondering where Ian Masters got $5,000 cash on St. Patrick's Day. Was it at all related to the shooting? Could Ian Masters have been the man in the mask?

At any rate, Fidelma had reluctantly agreed that they didn't have to tell Washington anything about ARM. That left Danny free to pursue the next line of inquiry he'd thought of before Fidelma had gotten kidnapped and thrown on his recliner: Kate McNamara Rodriguez, his past love, Joey's mother, and apparently Conway's lover.

So he'd called Detective Washington and asked the man about Kate's inheritance.

"Your girlfriend, Kate, got two hundred thousand from Conway," Washington had told him.

"She's not my girlfriend."

"Too bad," Washington said. "You could quit your teaching job if she was."

"So, is she a suspect?"

"The only suspect," Washington had informed him curtly, "is already in custody."

Danny said nothing, even though he wanted to yell at him about the autopsy report.

"Table for one?" the hostess at Rory Dolan's asked.

"Yes, please. And may I sit in Kate Rodriguez's section?"

The hostess hesitated, then glanced quickly at Danny. "Of course. Lucky you came. Tonight's her last night."

"Danny!" Kate exclaimed in surprise as she approached his table with the menu. "What are you doing here?"

Kate Rodriguez wore thick, rubber-soled black shoes, black twill pants, a white button-down shirt with bowtie and black apron. Her hair was pulled back from her face and knotted in a bun behind her head. Her face was the color of flour, her eyes and hair the color of coal. She wore three gold studs in one ear and bright purple lipstick.

"I'm here for dinner," he said pleasantly, "and maybe a word about Joey."

Kate looked back toward the kitchen. "Is something wrong?"

"Nothing serious."

As Kate handed Danny the menu, he noticed a snake slithering out of her right sleeve and across her fingers. A new tattoo. She had other tattoos that were not visible when she was dressed. Danny knew where they were—every one of them.

"Something to drink?"

"Bottled water."

"Perrier?" Kate asked, scribbling on her pad.

"Don't you have Poland Spring?" Danny quipped.

When Kate returned with the bottle of Perrier, Danny ordered the Dublin-style fish and chips. He handed back the menu. "Joey's a great kid. I know you're proud of him."

Kate heaved a sigh, tucked the menu under her arm, and blew a loose hair from her face. "He's a difficult child. He was always a high-needs kid, even as a baby. It's not easy raising him alone."

"I'm sure it's not. But you've been a good mother, Kate."

"Sometimes I wonder."

"There was a time when I thought I could be a good husband to you."

"We were kids then, Danny."

"We weren't *that* young."

"Neither one of us was ready for marriage."

"Well, sometimes I used to lay awake at night alone in my apartment—"

"Danny, don't—"

"Wondering what it would have been like if we *had* gotten married."

"That's ancient history."

Danny did not say that once he met Fidelma Muldoon, he rarely thought about that anymore.

"I better put your order in," Kate said, walking toward the kitchen.

Now he wondered if Kate were capable of gunning someone down—or paying someone else to do it. She was fiercely protective of her children and she would probably do just about anything to provide a secure future for them. For years now she had worked two jobs to give Joey the clothes and shoes so vital to a teen's self-esteem. But would she murder for him? Two hundred thousand dollars would buy a lot of shoes.

"I spoke to Joey about his work and his attitude on Monday," Danny began when Kate came back with the fish and chips and set it before him. "Do you have any idea what he plans to do when he graduates?"

Kate took a deep breath and let it out slowly. "I don't know. He doesn't tell me his plans."

"Has he thought about the Army?"

"Honestly, Danny, I don't know what Joey is thinking anymore."

"I'm afraid if he doesn't get to work he won't graduate at all. He needs time to study and do his homework."

A flicker of annoyance lit Kate's features. "Don't you think I know that? I've got two other kids to take care of and I'm working two jobs."

"I know, Kate. But Joey has to make it through this final year. He's so close, now."

"You don't have any idea what it's like raising three kids, do you?"

"I *do* understand how hard it is! But Joey's missed

a lot of classes this year. He's going to fail even *my* class if he doesn't start studying.'' Danny found himself slipping into their old argument pattern.

"I think Joey might be involved in some kind of criminal activity,'' Kate said. "I just can't control him anymore.''

Danny smoothed his mustache with his thumb and forefinger. "What kind of activity?''

"I'm not sure. He got in with the wrong crowd. He comes in at all hours, won't do a thing I tell him.'' Kate's voice cracked and she pulled a tissue from her apron pocket and held it to her nose. "He shows me no respect at all.''

"You're sounding a lot like our parents now, Kate. He's just a teenager.''

"It's different now. I'm afraid Joey could end up in serious trouble.''

"What kind of trouble?''

"I don't know. The night of St. Patrick's Day...'' Kate began.

"Yeah?''

"He came in late. He was upset. Hyper...like he was on some kind of drug.''

"Was he at the St. Patrick's Day parade?''

Kate laughed. "You've got to be kidding. Joey thinks all of that stuff is ridiculous. He relates to his Dominican roots more than to his Irish. He considers himself Latino.''

"He is.''

"And half Irish, too.''

Danny tried to lighten the conversation. "He's triple-hyphenated...Irish-Dominican-American.''

Kate smiled.

"What about you," Danny asked. "Did you go to the parade?"

She glanced quickly at Danny then looked away. "I was there, yeah, why?"

"Just curious. Did you see the grand marshal when he got shot?"

"Why all these questions? What are you trying to find out?"

"Relax, Kate. Nothing."

"I didn't see anything. I was nowhere near there."

"Hey, okay. Okay." Danny changed the subject. "The hostess tells me it's your last night here."

Kate looked at a spot over Danny's right shoulder. "That's right."

"How will you support yourself?"

"What business is that of yours?"

"Kate, I worry about you."

Kate rolled her eyes. "We'll get along." She glanced at the few people in the dining room. "Listen, I can't talk."

"Kate, I'm looking into a few things…"

"I'm busy, Danny."

"A few things about the death of Finn Conway."

The menu slipped from under Kate's arm and fell to the floor. She stared at Danny, not bothering to pick up the menu. "You what?"

"A friend of mine has been falsely accused of killing Conway. He's in Rikers Island right now. I'm trying to find out what's behind all this. I want to get him out."

Kate bent down and picked up the menu. "What's that have to do with me?"

"I know you were mentioned in his will."

She stood quickly, her eyes blazing. "That's none of your business, and who would tell you that?"

"I suppose none of it is any of my business," said Danny. "But I want to find out what happened to Fintan Conway. My friend's life is at stake."

Kate glanced back at the kitchen. "I can't talk here, Danny. I get off in half an hour. Meet me at the bar."

Danny finished his meal slowly, paid the check, found a secluded corner of the bar, and ordered a pint of Harp. He sipped slowly and thought about his student. He knew Joey would be all right in the long run. Joey would graduate from high school soon and either get a job or, hopefully, get into City College. Maybe he'd go for the Army. He'd settle down.

When Kate joined him, he ordered her a glass of Pinot Grigio.

"A few years back, Finn Conway came to me and offered to help us," Kate began without preamble. "I don't know why, really. He knew my husband was dead. Finn once helped my father out of a tight spot. Anyway, Conway has been helping us with money for several years. He was a good man. An extraordinary man. His enemies don't know the real man."

"Which enemies?"

"You know," Kate hesitated, looking around nervously. "Everyone who disagreed with him. Then about two months ago, Joey found out that I'd been getting money from Finn Conway. Joey went ballistic. I mean he totally lost control. I couldn't understand it. He accused me of all kinds of horrible things."

"Like what?"

"Like I might have had something to do with my

husband...his father's death. I don't know where he gets these crazy ideas.''

"Where do you think he's getting them?''

"I told you he's in with the wrong crowd. But he also said he'd talked to this man, Don Boyle, who knew all kinds of things about Tito.''

"What things?''

"I had no idea what he was talking about. He wouldn't give me any details. He hasn't talked to me since he found out Conway was giving us money. Then, when I found out this week that Conway left money to us in his will, I was completely shocked. I can't say anything to Joey about this. He wouldn't understand.''

"Kate?''

She looked at Danny. "What?''

"What *did* happen to your husband?''

Kate Rodriguez turned her wedding band nervously on her finger. "I don't know exactly. All I know is that he was not a drug dealer like he was made out to be.''

"You're sure?''

"Well, about a month before he was killed some men came to him. Told him they wanted him to give up his store. They wanted to rent it. But Tito had just signed a two-year lease. He had no intention of breaking his lease.''

"Why did the men want the store?''

"The store was right at the foot of the George Washington Bridge. Tito said the men were from Miami. He believed they probably wanted to use it as a drop-off point. Cars coming up Interstate Ninety-five from Miami could get off the GW Bridge and unload the stuff within seconds of arriving in the city. Then they could get back on the bridge and be on their way back to Miami, literally within minutes.''

"Drug dealers?''

"That's what Tito thought it was all about, because they offered him a lot of money. He was an honest man. He hated drugs and what they do to people.''

"I see.''

"Then about two weeks before he died, the landlord tried to force him out of the building. But like I said, he had just signed a two-year lease. He had no intention of moving. The landlord threatened him with all kinds of stuff but he held his ground. Two weeks later he was dead.''

"Who was the landlord?''

"I don't know. I really didn't get involved in Tito's business affairs. That's the way he wanted it. I took care of the kids, and he took care of business.''

Danny considered that for a long time, then took a sip of his pint. "Kate, Fintan Conway's wife believes you were having an affair with her husband.''

"I don't give a damn what she believes. He was helping us.'' Kate's hand shook as she picked up her glass of wine and took a sip. "That's all.''

"Why? Two hundred thousand dollars is a lot of help.''

Kate's left eyebrow twitched. "What's that supposed to mean?''

Danny looked down at his hands. "Kate, where were you on St. Patrick's Day?''

Kate missed the table as she tried to set down her wine, and the glass slipped and shattered on the floor. "What is this?'' she shrieked, ignoring the glass. "I already told you!''

"I'm just trying to account for everybody involved in this mess."

"Involved?" Kate's chest heaved. "*Involved?* What do you think, I put on a mask and shot Conway at the parade?"

Danny looked at her carefully. "Who said anything about a mask?"

"What?"

How did she know about the mask?

Kate stared at him for a long time. "It was in the paper. The police said they believed a masked gunman was involved."

"Forget it," Danny said. "Listen, do you want me to talk to Joey again? I think those hoods he's hanging around with near the subway tracks are his main problem."

"No." Kate put her hand on Danny's. "You're a good teacher. You've been a good role model for him. I'll take care of this. Now I have to go."

When Kate had gone, Danny stared into his glass. Did Kate really read about the mask in the newspaper? Besides, he had a hard time believing Finn Conway had given a substantial part of his estate to Kate Rodriguez just because he wanted to help her.

There had to be more to it than that.

TWENTY-FOUR

WHEN DANNY LOOKED UP from his pint, Fidelma Muldoon stood over him, a hurt expression on her face. "Who is she?"

"Who is who?" Danny turned his glass nervously. "What are you doing here?"

Fidelma glared at him.

Danny met her steady gaze and, after an awkward silence, said: "The mother of one of my students."

"Oh, really? Are you doing parent-teacher conferences in bars now?"

"Fidelma, this is serious."

"I'm sure 'tis."

"Her son is having some problems." Danny moved his pint aside. "What are *you* doing here?" he asked again.

"I'd a dinner meeting tonight, for your information."

"A date?" Danny asked, his heart sinking. "Who?"

"I got stood up, as you Yanks say."

"Who is he?" Or was Fidelma following him, too? Checking up on him? There was something else Danny wondered about. How did the people who broke into his apartment so easily get into the front door of the building and force Fidelma to walk up four flights of stairs without anyone noticing? After all, two masked gunmen walking up a stairway with a gun to a woman's head would certainly draw attention, even in Danny's neighborhood. Was it even remotely possible that Fidelma was involved with ARM? Could she have been in on the murder and intentionally led Danny astray? Had she let them in?

Danny shook his head to chase these thoughts away. After all, he loved Fidelma. Was he going crazy? What was he thinking? Things were getting out of control. These were completely crazy, paranoid, bizarre thoughts too terrible to contemplate. But Danny contemplated them anyway. "Who is he, Fidelma?"

"He's a *girl*," she said. "I met her through work." Fidelma knitted her brow and the corners of her mouth turned down. "I'm still shaking from when those hooligans dragged me into your apartment."

"It was pretty scary."

"What's wrong with this woman's son?"

Danny considered Fidelma's question. He really cared about Joey, not just because he had once loved Joey's mother, but because he understood the pain of losing a father. Even though his own father had died when Danny was thirty-eight, he still understood what a blow it must have been for Joey to lose his father at just eleven. It seemed that every man wanted his father's approval. When a man loses his father early, he still wants that approval but there's no one there to give it.

"He's just a teenager," Danny said, "who's been raised without a father. But there's something else: I think his mother, Kate, may be mixed up in Conway's murder somehow."

"Who is she, Danny?" she asked again, sitting down. Fidelma's eyes shifted nervously around the room.

Danny took another sip from his pint and reached over and put his hand on Fidelma's. "Someone I grew up with in the neighborhood. We went to high school together."

Fidelma stiffened and moved her hand from beneath Danny's. "You loved her, didn't you?"

"A long time ago. Yes."

"I'll be going," she said abruptly.

"Fidelma, please. Let me buy you a drink."

"Is that the line you use with all your girls?"

"Oh, for the love of—"

Fidelma smiled. "Sure, I'm only codding you. It's just that I keep thinking about those people from ARM. I tried to sleep this afternoon, but I woke up screaming when I remembered them holding a gun to my head." She shuddered slightly as she let out her breath. "I don't know how much longer I can stay in New York after what happened. This place is an urban jungle. I want to go home."

"Well, you know now they weren't really going to hurt us," he commented lamely, skirting the threat of her leaving.

"They held a gun to my head!"

"You can stay at my place if you need company."

"I'll think about it."

"Or maybe you can call some friends who'll let you stay over. You shouldn't be alone."

Fidelma said nothing.

"I just hope those people from ARM *can* help Brendan in some way."

"I called Brendan's family," Fidelma said.

"How are they holding up?"

"Not well. They're scared out of their minds for Brendan."

"I'll bet."

"Now, tell me what you've found out about Conway." Fidelma brought herself under control and smiled wanly. "And tell me how your ex-love is involved?"

"Knock it off, Fidelma. Actually, there are quite a few people involved. First of all there's this guy from Belfast named Ian Masters. He's a singer in a band with Brendan. The first time I talked to Masters he said a green Mercedes had picked Brendan up after their gig at O'Dwyer's the night before St. Patrick's Day."

"Those people in the green Mercedes who nearly killed us in your apartment," Fidelma whispered. "They were with Brendan the night before the shooting, so."

"They didn't nearly kill us, Fidelma."

"Sure, I still don't trust them."

"There's more," Danny went on. "I found out that Ian Masters paid a studio five thousand dollars on St. Patrick's Day to record an album."

"So what?"

"Doesn't it make you wonder where he got that kind of money?" Danny asked.

"Not really. How do you know how much money this fellow has? Maybe he inherited it. Stole it years ago. A gift from a fan. Maybe he's just frugal, Danny."

"I don't know. If you met this guy, Masters, you'd wonder where he got the money, too. But okay, maybe you're right. He's independently wealthy. He just looks like he doesn't know where his next meal is coming from because it fits his image of a down-and-out rocker. But I'm still checking on him. Anyway, remember Matt Gill, Conway's son? His father basically disowned him because he's gay.''

"How sad.''

"Just before he was killed, Fintan Conway planned to cut his son, Matt, out of his will.''

"You think his own son may have killed him so he wouldn't be disinherited?''

"It's possible. I *do* know that Matt Gill's partner, Cedric Powers, is chairman of GILA and that Matt borrowed a high-powered rifle with a scope from his father's gun case to loan to Powers to use for a play—or so says his mother.''

Even as he said it, Danny had dismissed the high-powered rifle theory of the grand marshal's murder. It was clear from the autopsy report that Conway was shot from ground level. But Danny did wonder about the gun.

"Who did he loan it to?''

"I told you, to Cedric Powers.''

"Really. Anything else?''

"Quite a bit, actually. Speaking of Matt's mother, Maureen Conway herself had an excellent reason to kill her husband, since she believed he was having an affair.''

"She couldn't have killed him. She was walking beside her husband in the parade.''

"She could have *paid* someone to shoot him.''

"And who is this woman Conway was having an affair with?'' asked Fidelma. "Maybe *she* was involved.''

Fidelma had voiced Danny's worst fear and somehow hearing her say it made Danny realize how absolutely logical it was that Kate Rodriguez might have murdered Conway for his money. Hearing Fidelma say it suddenly gave it an unwelcomed legitimacy.

"Just some woman," Danny mumbled.

"Who?"

Danny whispered, "The woman you just saw sitting here."

"Aha!"

"Now, Fidelma…"

"And you're trying to protect her?" Fidelma's voice rose. "Aren't you?"

"That's not true."

"She was the one in the mask you saw. You said something flashed in the masked person's hand."

"I don't want to jump to any conclusions before I get the facts."

"You sound so pompous! Well, what facts *do* you have?"

"She inherited some money from Conway when he died."

Fidelma sat back and crossed her arms over her chest. "How convenient."

"Who's sounding pompous now?" Danny asked. "Besides, there's someone else we haven't really considered, isn't there?"

"Sure, and who might that be?"

"Fidelma," Danny began gently. "Do you think maybe the police could be right?"

"What in the world are you talking about?"

"Maybe Brendan *did* have something to do with Conway's death, even if he didn't shoot him from the Plaza."

"How can you say that?" Fidelma gasped. "Brendan wouldn't hurt a soul."

"I think maybe he's been involved in hurting souls for a long time now. After all, he's been with ARM for over ten years. Maybe they were afraid I was going to find something out and they wanted to put me off the trail. How do we know they were telling us the truth?"

"We don't know what Brendan did with ARM." She looked across the room and frown lines wrinkled her brow. "Besides, why would *they* kill Conway? He was no threat to them."

"I just don't know."

"I thought you were the big detective."

Blood rushed to Danny's face. "You're the one who talked me into getting involved in this whole mess. Now I might even lose my job because I'm so caught up in all this, and you're talking about moving back to Ireland! What about us?"

"What do you mean, lose your job?"

"The principal told me I've been missing too much school."

"That's not my fault. You make your own decisions."

Danny ignored the remark and turned his pint glass in his hand. "Then there's the chairman of the parade committee—Don Boyle. He used to be a close friend of the Conways. But he hated Fintan. Said he was the worst choice for grand marshal the parade committee ever made."

"Why?"

"Too controversial, I guess. Besides, Fintan Conway was disrupting their meetings," Danny hesitated a moment. "Kate just said her son, Joey, had talked to Boyle, too. Strange. Anyway, Conway wanted the parade committee to be held accountable to the whole membership of the Ancient Order of Hibernians. He said they made too many decisions without the participation of the membership. But you know there's something else that's odd about this whole business. Mo Conway said her husband was taken off life support and then he died. He had signed a living will.''

''What's odd about that? Loads of people sign those things now.''

''Well, I told you I went to the *New York Voice* and read nearly every column Conway ever wrote. In several of the columns he made it clear he was opposed to euthanasia.''

''Taking a person off life support is not euthanasia, Danny.''

''Conway wrote that he was opposed even to taking people off life support.''

''But why?''

''Because of the opportunity for abuse. Conway believed it opened the door to other kinds of killing. If you could legally terminate the life of the incurably ill, then what next? The criminally insane? The severely handicapped?''

''I guess I've never looked at it like that.''

''I just don't believe,'' Danny said, ''that Fintan Conway would have ever voluntarily signed a living will.''

''Well, why don't you find a copy of the will? Maybe talk to the family or judge or whoever allowed the doctors to take him off life support.''

''That's exactly what I'm planning to do.''

TWENTY-FIVE

IT WAS FRIDAY, March 30th, the end of a rough week at school. All week, Dr. Zamora had watched Danny intently. Nearly two weeks had passed since the St. Patrick's Day murder of Fintan Conway. Joey Rodriguez had been belligerent all week and cursed Danny in front of the class for no apparent reason. Later, Joey had shoved another kid against a locker, badly bruising the boy's head. Then today, Joey had been absent from school altogether.

When school let out, Danny went to see Maureen Conway, who gave him a copy of the living will, which he took downtown to a professional document examiner in Midtown. Then he found a phone in the back of the Blarney Star on Eighth Avenue and called information. Danny wanted to find out who had owned the building on 178th and Broadway where Tito Rodriguez had been killed. But he wasn't sure how to go about it. He knew, of course, that the ownership of property was recorded but didn't know where exactly—the county clerk's office, the hall of records?

"Can you give me the general information number for City Government?" he asked the operator.

He dialed the number, then punched his way through half a dozen recorded commands that reminded him of a joke he'd recently heard about an HMO hotline: "If you're having a heart attack, please press one…"

Finally he got through to the Department of Finance at the City Collector's Office, the office that mails the real estate tax bills.

"I'm sorry," the clerk told him, "we can't give that kind of information over the phone. If you'd like to come down here, we'll see what we can find."

But Danny didn't have time. Instead, he raced downtown on the 1 Train to the Flatiron Building to talk with Mr. Zhang again. As the train pulled into 23rd Street, Danny saw the subway platform packed with commuters already going home. They piled into the open doors of the train as Danny pushed his way off. More commuters marched down the stairs of the station like an army of ants with briefcases.

Danny got out of the train and climbed the steps of the subway. Outside, the sky was the color of oatmeal. As Danny stepped onto 23rd Street a vicious crosswind knifed him in the back. Danny buttoned his overcoat, tugged on his Donegal tweed cap, and walked east toward Madison Square. The wind whipped across Broadway, sending an empty plastic garbage bag swirling into the air. It floated back and forth like a kite, then dove, hitting a businessman who snatched it angrily away and tossed it back into the air.

Then Danny had an idea. He stopped at a pay phone and dialed his Aunt Bertie's office.

"Another favor?" she asked.

"Yes. And thanks for the autopsy report."

"I don't know what you're talking about."

"The report—"

"Let's just say neither one of us ever saw that... okay?"

"Right. Now, Bert. Is there any way you can find out for me who owns number Eighty-five, One Hundred and Seventy-eighth Street? That's near the corner of One-seventy-eighth and Broadway. I need to know who owned the building in nineteen ninety-five. I just called the Department of Finance at the City Collector's Office, but I don't have time to go there right now."

"No problem," said Aunt Bertie in a surprisingly cooperative tone. "I can have a tax certiorari attorney tap into the city system and get all the details."

"Excellent! Can you leave a message on my machine?"

"Done deal."

Danny found Mr. Zhang in Archives and Research on the 8th floor, having coffee. "Yes, Fintan Conway confided in me on many occasions," Mr. Zhang admitted. "But as complicated as Finn was, he really had a very simple dream."

"What was that?"

"He just wanted to go back to Ireland and live out his final years with his wife on some land they owned over there."

"When was he planning to retire?"

"In just a few years, I think," Mr. Zhang said.

"I see."

"Can I get you a coffee?" Mr. Zhang asked.

"I'd love one."

They sipped their coffees. Since Mr. Zhang had done research for Conway, Danny figured he might know a lot more about him than his colleagues. "Did you do any research for Conway related to a man named Tito Rodriguez?''

Zhang tipped his head to one side and shut his left eye. "I don't remember that name."

"He was an alleged drug dealer who was murdered in nineteen ninety-five. Conway wrote a column about him."

"Can't say that I remember anything about it."

"What about the holy mountain in Ireland, Croagh Patrick? Did Conway ever mention that to you?"

"Oh, yes." Mr. Zhang nodded vigorously, apparently glad he could finally be of help. "He was very interested in that story. That's what he was working on the week he was killed."

"Really? Do you have anything on that?"

Mr. Zhang glanced at a file cabinet. "All Mr. Conway's notes are sealed now."

Danny looked at his watch. "Is there any way I could take a quick look?"

"I'm afraid not."

Danny shook Mr. Zhang's hand. "Thanks for your help."

"Sorry I couldn't do more."

Mr. Zhang turned out the lights and followed Danny to the elevator. Danny pushed the button for the lobby and Mr. Zhang pushed 7.

"Thanks again," Danny said as Zhang got off on his floor.

Danny pushed the button for the second floor, where he got off. Then he caught a rising elevator back to the 8th floor. Danny's heart fluttered when the elevator stopped again at 7 and the doors opened. Zhang stood there, his back to the elevator door, talking to a woman.

Danny backed into a corner of the elevator as the woman got on. Zhang turned just as the doors were closing and Danny hoped the clerk hadn't seen him.

To his dismay, the woman got off with him on the 8th floor. She walked briskly up the hall. Danny made directly for the Archives and Research door, but it was locked. As he looked around, the woman stopped and turned. "Can I help you with something?" She glanced around nervously as if afraid to be alone with Danny in the corridor.

"Oh, I left something inside."

"Alex Zhang's down on seven. He'll have to let you in."

Danny hesitated.

"I haven't seen you before," she said. "Do you work here?"

"I don't work for the paper, no. Mr. Zhang was showing me the Archives and Research department."

She looked at him skeptically. "Well, he'll have to let you back in."

"I'm a teacher," Danny blurted. "I'm working journalism into my Social Studies classes. I thought I'd bring them for a field trip to Archives and Research."

The wrinkles on her brow vanished and she smiled. "What a wonderful idea! I have two kids in high school. I never thought of Archives and Research for a field trip. Here, I'll let you in." She fished a card key from her pocket and waved it in front of what looked like a speaker beside the door.

"You should bring them to the newsroom, too," said the woman.

"Thanks," Danny said as the door clicked open.

He stepped inside, his pulse racing. "Thanks again." Danny waited nervously for her to leave.

But she stayed put, watching him.

"Let's see, where did I leave those keys? Thanks, again, I'll find them."

"I'll wait."

Just then her cell phone beeped and she plucked it from her purse. "Yes. Yes. I'm right here for goodness' sake. In Archives. All right, all right. Gotta go," she said to Danny. "Turn off the lights when you're finished. The door locks automatically behind you."

He heard her heels ticking as she walked away down the hall.

The room was completely dark and as Danny felt along the wall for a light switch he crashed into a chair. The chair tipped over, making a bang that sounded like it would bring everyone in the building running.

Danny froze, the pulse in his temples throbbing. He continued feeling along the wall for the switch. When he found it, he flicked it on, flooding the room with brightness. When his eyes adjusted, he moved to the bank of files Zhang had glanced at when Danny asked about the Croagh Patrick story. As he reached for the first file drawer the office door swung open.

Danny spun around to face the woman who had returned.

"Oh," he said, holding his hand over his heart. "You scared me."

She examined him for a moment. "Did you find it?"

"Find what?"

Her eyes probed Danny as if trying to size him up. "Whatever you left behind?" she asked.

"Oh, yeah." He slapped his pockets. "Left my keys. Got them. Now I'm looking for my reading glasses."

She smiled, walked toward him, and handed him a business card. "I think it's such a great idea about bringing the class. If you want to give them a tour of the newsroom, just give me a call."

Danny took the card. "I will."

When she left, Danny went back to the file cabinet and opened it. He rifled through the files, suddenly struck by the futility of such a search. There were hundreds of files in just this drawer and there were dozens of drawers. He didn't even know what he was looking for, and it wasn't clear how things were filed. Danny rifled frantically through one drawer after another. In the fourth cabinet, he came up with a fat folder bulging with papers. When he opened it, the first thing he saw was a print-out from the Internet of a story originally published in the *Irish Times* concerning the discovery of gold on Croagh Patrick. He glanced through the rest of the file and found other clippings and handwritten notes concerning gold on Croagh Patrick. He found a scrap of paper where Fintan Conway—apparently—had scribbled: "Church approved of mining?"

Danny looked around for a copy machine. He'd copy the file and examine it more closely later. Just as he turned on the copier he heard the door, which had automatically locked from the outside behind him, click open.

He ducked behind the copier just as Zhang walked into the office. The clerk craned his neck, apparently surprised that the light was on, and scratched his forehead. He walked over to one of the desks and picked up a folder, walked to the door, and snapped off the light.

Danny let out his breath.

But Zhang didn't leave the room. Danny could hear his breathing. That's when Danny noticed the glow of the copy machine.

"What's that doing on?" Zhang asked himself out loud. He flicked the light back on and walked to the copier, where Danny sat crouched, hiding.

"Strange," Zhang murmured and turned off the copier.

When he finally left, Danny stood up and took a deep breath, trying to slow his racing heart.

He reached into the folder, removed half of the clippings—faxes from Ireland and other correspondence—and turned on the copier again. When it was warmed up, he started copying frantically.

In ten minutes he'd made a copy of the entire file. He returned the original to its place in the cabinet, turned off the copier, turned out the light, and stuck his head out the door to see if anyone was in the hall. When he was sure he was alone, he slipped out, walked briskly to the elevator and pushed the down arrow.

It seemed to take forever for the elevator to come. When it did, Danny stepped inside and pushed the button for the lobby. He heaved a sigh of relief as the elevator descended. Then, just as he thought he was safe, the elevator stopped on the 7th floor and Mr. Zhang stepped in.

Danny moved against the wall and held the file behind his back with one hand.

"What are you doing here?" Zhang asked, his eyes narrowed.

Danny reached his free hand into his top pocket, took out the business card and glanced at it. "I was talking to...Janet Mason."

"I thought you left the building?"

"No, I had a meeting with her, too."

Zhang scratched his head. "I don't think she knew Conway very well."

"No," Danny said. "I realize that now. Waste of time, I guess." The elevator had stopped at the lobby. "Thanks again for your help."

Mr. Zhang looked at him oddly as Danny dashed from the building.

TWENTY-SIX

"YOU AGAIN?" Ian Masters said as Danny approached.

Danny had shoved his way through the crowd that spilled out the front door of O'Neil's Pub on 3rd Avenue and 48th Street. Standing three deep at the bar, the place was so jammed with people they could hardly move. When the band took a break, Danny elbowed his way up for a drink just as two people stepped away, leaving enough space to shoe-horn himself into a standing position beside Ian Masters at the mahogany bar. Danny placed the file folder next to him.

"You must be happy for your mate, then," Masters said.

"Who?"

"Brendan Grady. Haven't you heard?"

"No. What?"

Three bartenders pulled pints of Guinness and beer as fast as they could. Danny shouted for a Harp.

Masters took a swig of his own Guinness and looked down at Danny as if he held a Royal Flush and Danny had turned up three of a kind. "It's been all over the news."

Ironically, Danny hadn't seen the news all day.

He'd been busy with school and had missed the evening news the night before, too.

"What are you talking about?"

"Quite the daredevil, your man Brendan."

The bartender set a Harp in front of Danny. The barman had the bright red face, jet black hair, and milk-white hands of an Irishman, and a voice that had the Bronx written all over it. "Five bucks."

"What happened?" Danny asked as he slapped a twenty on the bar.

Masters chuckled, sipped from his pint, set it in front of him and settled back as if ready to tell a good yarn. "According to the *New York Voice,* Brendan got sick about five p.m. yesterday. Vomited and complained of stomach cramps. The guards thought he had food poisoning—or had been poisoned—so they moved him to the infirmary." Masters paused, obviously waiting for some response from Danny.

Danny found Masters' posturing annoying. "Go on," he said. He reminded Danny of Garda Kelley, the cop back in Ireland—who held every scrap of information as if it were a precious gem and doled it out piece by piece.

"He was there until seven p.m.," Ian went on. "After he had dinner, he vomited again and started screaming. Two Corrections Officers came in, strapped him to a gurney, and wheeled him to another building. On the way, two of Brendan's mates jumped the COs, changed into their clothes, and tied them up. In the meantime a third member of the gang hijacked a prison ambulance."

Danny shook his head, truly amazed at the efficiency with which ARM had worked. To have gotten into a high-security institution like Rikers Island was amazing; to pull something like this off...a miracle. Either that or an inside job.

"They loaded Brendan into the ambulance and drove to the north end of Rikers Island where a speed boat waited."

"Really? A speed boat?"

"Right. I guess your mate, Brendan, is a lot better connected than I thought he was. The speed boat raced out into Long Island Sound. The Coast Guard believes there was a fishing trawler or a yacht waiting for them. They're staking out ports in Ireland where it's most likely they'll try to take him. But, sure, they could take him anywhere. Why not Spain? Korea. Timbuktu."

"Timbuktu is landlocked."

"Whatever."

"How do you know all this?"

"It was just on *New York One*. You should watch more TV."

Danny bit back the urge to tell Masters to shove it. Instead, he feigned disinterest and switched subjects. "How did the recording session go?"

"The what? Oh." Masters smiled. "Could have been better. But, sure, I laid down some great tracks."

What an egotist.

An attractive brunette stood near Masters and he eyed her crudely and asked, "What's your sign?"

She gave the singer a withering look. "Do Not Enter!"

Danny chuckled. "What are you calling the album?"

"Screw You!"

"Hey," Danny said. "I'm just curious."

"Screw You!" Masters repeated. "That's the name of the album."

"I see." Danny smiled. "Catchy title, that." He hesitated a second. "Tell me, how much does something like that cost?"

"Something like what?"

"A recording session."

"What's it to you?"

"Let me put it this way. The recording session cost you five thousand bucks. You paid in cash up front. I know for a fact that you had twenty-six dollars and fifty cents to your name the day before St. Patrick's."

"You don't know how much money I have," Masters said, but his voice lacked conviction.

"I had a friend of mine who is talented in that area hack into your bank account records. She found out that the day before St. Patrick's Day your account balance suddenly went up to five thousand twenty-six dollars and fifty cents. Now, I'm curious about where you got that kind of money." Beat. "On St. Patrick's Day."

For the first time since Danny had met him, Ian Masters was speechless. Then, Masters reached out and snatched Danny by the lapels and jerked his face toward his own twisted, enraged features. "Look, you dweeb, I don't know what you're up to, but you stay the bloody hell out of my bloody business, you got that?"

Danny removed Masters' hands from his lapels and straightened his tie. "Touch a raw nerve, did I?"

"I ought to have you busted for tampering with my bank account," Masters shouted. "I had nothing to do with the murder of Conway."

"Who said anything about murder?"

"Well...well..." Masters stuttered, lowering his voice. "That's what you're snooping around all the time about, ain't it?"

"So, you don't want to tell me how you came up with five thousand dollars?"

"How I make my money is my business, mate."

"It might be police business as well," Danny put his hand around his pint.

"You threatening me?"

"Not at all. I'm just thinking that you might have information about Brendan's whereabouts on St. Patrick's Day that would interest the police. And by the way, where were *you* at one-fifty p.m. on St. Patrick's Day?"

"So bloody hung over I couldn't get out of bed."

"Poor baby." Danny took a sip and put his glass down. "Can someone verify that?"

"I don't need to verify anything for you, mate. Why don't you just face it. Your killer friend, Brendan, murdered Conway and his Fenian terrorist mates broke him out of jail."

Danny had held himself back since the day he met Ian Masters. Maybe it was the investigation, the ugly suspicion that Brendan just might be guilty, Joey Rodriguez's troubles, the stress, or just Ian Masters' crappy attitude, but something inside Danny shattered. He grabbed Masters by the shirt collar and twisted it until the singer's face turned purple.

"You're choking me," Masters gasped.

Danny grabbed Masters' arm and wrenched it behind his back. The bar was so crowded that as Danny put his lips to Masters' ear, most people in the bar probably thought they were just having a private conversation. "I'll rip your larynx out through your nostrils,'' Danny hissed with uncharacteristic violence as he turned Masters' arm. ''You tell me what you know about this whole business.''

''Look, mate, I'm gonna give you something,'' Masters squeaked. ''Then I want you to stay out of my face!''

''How can I stay away?'' Danny asked, putting pressure on Masters' arm. ''I'm your biggest fan.''

''Someone came to me,'' Ian began breathlessly, his face screwed into a grimace.

Danny relaxed the hold on Masters' collar so he could talk and increased the pressure on his arm.

''Two nights before St. Patrick's Day. I had a solo gig at Paddy Reilly's.''

''On Second Avenue?''

''That's the one. Anyway, during a break this bloke comes up and asks do I play in a band with Brendan Grady. I do, says I. Dead Leper Cons. What of it? He says, 'How'd you like to make some money—a lot of money.' I says I'm always in need of a little extra boodle. He says, 'Good.' He tells me to phone in an anonymous tip to Crimestoppers Hotline before the St. Patrick's Day parade. 'Tell them the fellow who plays in your band—Brendan Grady—is talking about wasting the grand marshal of the parade. If they convict him,' he tells me, 'you'll get a reward from the cops, as well.' ''

''He wanted you to finger Brendan?'' Danny remembered Washington saying that a tip had been phoned in just minutes before the shooting.

''I needed the cash.''

''You shithead,'' Danny said, twisting his arm again. This time he heard a bone pop and several people looked at them when Masters screamed. "You sent an innocent man to jail."

"He's out."

Danny let him go. Masters' arm hung at a crazy angle from his shoulder. "He's free," Masters said, rubbing his throat with his good hand. "You broke my bloody arm."

Danny's whole body shook. "Can you identify the guy who gave you the money?"

"What's it worth to you?"

Danny reached out to grab his arm again and Masters backed away. "Okay, okay. I found out later who he was."

"Tell me."

"His name's Boyle. Donald Boyle."

TWENTY-SEVEN

DANNY MADE A QUICK CALL to 411 to get Boyle's address, called his own home phone number and listened to the messages on his message machine. The first was from Aunt Bertie. The building at 178th and Broadway was owned in 1995 by Donald Boyle. He sold it in 1997 to an apartment management company based in Miami. The second message was from the document examiner.

Danny listened, then raced out of the bar. Needles of icy rain pricked his face and the reflection of lights blinked in the slick street. Sirens moaned in the distance and the humid chill razored through Danny's jacket as he flagged a cab on 3rd Avenue.

"Get on the FDR," he told the handsome young man in a purple turban sitting behind the wheel. "And head uptown."

"Congratulations, sir. You are my very first customer as a driver of taxicabs."

"Oh, no!"

"Now tell me, please, what is FDR?"

"Turn here," Danny instructed, and they raced east on 46th Street, the wipers of the cab slapping back and forth, marking time.

Danny glanced nervously at the cabby, who stared

at him in the rearview mirror as they moved into heavy traffic.

Finally, the cabby asked, "Are you happy, sir?"

"What?"

"I sense that you are deeply troubled," the cab-driver said. "Perhaps you are seeking something you have been unable to find."

Or someone? Danny could see the cabby's eyes examining him in the rearview mirror. He glanced at his ID taped to the back of the bullet-proof Plexiglas partition between them: Ravi Ajmera. Of all the cabs in the city, Danny had to flag an Indian philosopher. "Turn here onto the highway. Up that ramp."

"Very good, sir."

"No, I'm not happy."

"I suspected as much, sir. Have you tried deep breathing?"

"New York 101," Danny said when they were on the highway speeding north, "this is the Franklin D. Roosevelt Drive, also known as the FDR—named for our president who served from nineteen thirty-three to nineteen forty-five."

"Oh, yes, yes. The New Deal. Very great man, sir. Friend of the poor man like our Ghandi. Very wise on the domestic scene. But he gave too much to the Soviets at Yalta, I'm afraid." The cabby smiled as if FDR's shortcomings delighted him.

"The FDR runs up the east side of Manhattan," continued Danny. "Its counterpart on the west is the West Side Highway."

"You must be a school teacher," said the cabby, "the way you lecture."

The lights of Roosevelt Island twinkled like a trea-sure chest of gems that had been spilled in a hasty getaway on its shores. Danny saw the swaying carriages of the tram pass overhead carrying commuters to the island.

"That's the Queensboro Bridge," Danny said, pointing through the smeared window to the string of lights connecting Manhattan and Queens.

"The city is beautiful. So beautiful."

Yes it is, Danny thought. Viewed from the FDR at night, it was a city of a million lights and spires—highrises that poked into the wet, inky night—and a city of a million dreams. Still the magnet for the hungry and ambitious who came from every corner of the globe to prove themselves. The cabdriver was probably a lawyer or a professor back home, waiting now for a break.

"Do you wish to talk, sir?"

Did he ever. "It's been a long day. I just broke a man's arm."

"Relax. Deep breath," the cabby instructed. "Now let it all go."

Danny directed the cabdriver onto the Major Deegan Expressway. "That's not all," said Danny. "A good friend of mine is accused of a crime he didn't commit. Now I just found out he broke out of prison." Why was he telling the cabdriver all of this? he wondered.

"We all want to be free," said the cabby.

"Of course we do. But if he's innocent I could have helped him get free."

"You can neither give nor take away your friend's freedom. Walls, blocks, and bars do not imprison us. Our compulsions imprison us."

"Turn here," said Danny, and they drove into the Bainbridge section of the Bronx.

"Look at me," the cabby went on. "If I am to succeed as a cabdriver I will have to spend many, many hours a day, six days a week behind this wheel. I have less space than your friend had in his prison cell. I must work these long hours to buy food and shelter for my wife and children. I must send money as well to my mother and father in India. Some would say I am not a free man. They would be wrong. The mind and the spirit—they are not locked inside this cab with me."

"Okay."

"And you, sir. I can see from your eyes that you are not free. Your mind is cluttered with problems. You are looking for something—for someone. This is a problem you feel compelled to solve. But when you solve that problem, two more problems will take its place. And your mind will be more cluttered than before. A cluttered, worried, agitated mind can never find a solution because it is incapable of seeing the problem."

"What do you mean?"

The cab bounced through a series of potholes.

"Only when your mind is free can you see the world clearly. When the sea is rough and agitated, you cannot see the fish, the sand, the coral. But when the sea is calm and peaceful you can see everything clearly."

Danny told the cabby to turn right.

"I think your friend missed a great opportunity," said the cabby.

"Uh...excuse me?"

"Most people are imprisoned by their own needs. We need food for our families. We need shelter, we need clean water. Our minds are crowded with problems that result from trying to fulfill these needs. And so we are not free. Our minds are not free and our hours are filled with searching for solutions to our problems.''

He's right, thought Danny.

''On the other hand, all of your friend's needs were being provided in jail. He had food and shelter and fresh water provided for him. Perhaps for the first time in his life he had the capacity to free himself. His mind could be at rest and like the sea that is calm and quiet he could have looked deeply within himself.''

''He was behind bars! At Rikers Island,'' Danny practically screamed. ''Do you know what Rikers Island is like?''

''It is of no consequence. You are agitated again. Now, I ask you, when your friend had the serenity to look within himself you know what he might have seen?''

''No, you tell me.''

''There he may have glimpsed the face of God.''

When they pulled in front of Boyle's rowhouse on 204th Street, the block was filled with cop cars, their red lights flashing. Danny opened the door of the cab and handed the cabby an extra big tip.

''We are the prisoners,'' said the cabby. ''Your friend had the opportunity to be free.''

Danny stepped out of the cab. ''Good luck to you.''

''Be happy,'' he said to Danny. ''Remember, you are your deepest driving desire.''

The rain fell in torrents now, and Danny stood without an umbrella in the doorway of the cab, listening. ''What your desire is, so is your will. What your will is, so is your deed. What your deed is, so is your destiny.''

"Says who?" asked Danny.

"It is from the Upanishads."

"Thanks," Danny said, and the cab disappeared into the Bronx.

Danny ran up the stairs of Boyle's house. The first thing he noticed was the door ajar.

Not bothering to knock, he pushed open the door.

"Hey, you can't come in here," said a cop stationed just inside the door.

A man in a dark business suit, his back to Danny, hung by his neck from a length of lamp cord tied to an overhead radiator pipe in the kitchen. The smashed lamp hung beside him and the toes of the man's wingtips scraped the floor. The mask pushed roughly over his head had been twisted backward so that Danny stared into the garish leer of a stage Irishman—thick eyebrows and mustache, bulbous red nose and ears.

Five police officers stood among the smashed dishes, broken chairs, and flipped tables. The apartment looked as though a bull had raged through it. One officer took snapshots of the body from several angles while another cop scribbled into his notebook. A third made measurements with a tape.

A man in a gray trenchcoat turned to face Danny.

"O'Flaherty! What are you doing here?" asked Detective Washington.

TWENTY-EIGHT

WHEN THEY TOOK the body down and removed the mask, Don Boyle stared up at them, his eyes bulging from their sockets, his purple tongue protruding from his mouth. His swollen face was red as Bloody Mary mix, and his throat black and blue where the lamp cord had dug into it. A bloody froth clung to his lips and tongue. His head rolled sideways, neck broken.

"What are you doing here?" Washington asked again. He called to another officer. "Take over here for a minute."

Danny shifted the bulging file of Conway's columns to his other hand and stared in shock at the body now on the floor.

"You were right about the guy in the mask," Washington said. "Looks like he did shoot Conway."

Danny surveyed the gruesome scene, speechless.

"You think this was a suicide?" Washington poked his chin in the direction of the body. A technician had taken down the victim's pants and was placing a thermometer in his rectum.

"What in the name of..." Danny said, aghast.

"We're getting a body temperature, O'Flaherty," Washington said nonchalantly. "When we compare body temperature to room temperature we can get a rough idea of when Boyle cashed in his chips."

"When did you find him?" asked Danny.

Washington looked at his watch. "Not long ago. We checked his temp as soon as we got here. Doing it again, now. We did a walk-through of the apartment and organized a command post in the bedroom. There's a telephone in there. We've done a preliminary survey. Now we're recording and collecting evidence, so don't touch anything. Did you see a white Ford Expedition out front? I'm waiting for the medical examiner."

"No. I don't think so. Where's Boyle's wife?"

"Neighbors said she went out of town a couple days ago."

"Boyle didn't kill Conway," Danny said.

Detective Washington rolled his eyes. "Remember what I told you about police work?"

"Yeah. Forensics, right?"

"That's right. Let me tell you how we found the guy in the mask. First we tracked down three different news crews that covered the parade that day. Dedicated, hard-working police officers put in over three hundred man-hours going over those tapes frame by frame. Finally, we found a tape that had your masked man. He appeared on tape for less than a second and all we had was a quarter of the mask and an image of the feet. The photo lab blew up that one frame from the video into an eight-by-ten photographic still. We identified the brand and style of the shoes, but got nowhere with that. Then we tracked down the manufacturer of the mask."

"Very impressive, Detective."

"That ain't half of it. Officers spent another hundred hours going through photographs of public events where Conway was pictured. We were working on a theory that whoever knocked him off knew him in some professional capacity.''

"I thought you were working on a theory that someone shot him from the ninth floor of the Plaza Hotel?''

"Yeah, right. Not even *you* bought that one.''

Washington called to a female officer with a diagram pad. "I want sketches of the exits, too. All of them.'' He turned back to Danny. "So, anyway, we took photos of a couple dozen different people who were frequently seen with Conway, including Boyle, and went to every single retail outlet in the New York area that sold theatrical supplies. A woman at a shop in Jersey City ID'd Boyle as the guy who bought the mask. Said she was positive enough to testify to it in court.''

Washington waited for Danny to say something. When he didn't, the police detective added, "That's how the bad guys get caught, O'Flaherty. Painstaking, methodical investigation.''

"What about the story?''

"What story?''

Danny held up the file. "*Why* he did it.''

"Detective work is inductive, O'Flaherty. We draw conclusions from specific facts called evidence. We take the evidence—the facts of the case—and construct a theory of the crime from those available facts. It doesn't work the other way around. Evidence has to speak for itself in court. Everybody there has a *story*.''

"Boyle didn't kill Conway. You know that as well as I do. Boyle was on the reviewing stand in clear sight of hundreds of people when the grand marshal was shot. He didn't kill him.''

"And now you're as sure about him as you were about Brendan Grady?" Washington asked. "You're a real piece of work, O'Flaherty."

"And don't try to tell me this was a suicide. You want me to believe Boyle trashed his apartment before he put a mask on backward and hung himself with a lamp cord?"

"Then you know who did this?"

"I'll show you."

TWENTY-NINE

WASHINGTON TOOK a blue light from under the driver's seat and attached it to the roof of his unmarked '98 Chevy Lumina. Danny flipped through the file as they raced across Van Cortland Park, turned left on Broadway, and sped across the Broadway Bridge into Upper Manhattan with lights flashing.

Conway had scribbled a note in the margin of a printed e-mail from someone in Dublin: "DB might harm the woman or her children if they find out."

"This better be good, O'Flaherty. I've just left a team of men and women back at a crime scene. A NYPD homicide detective doesn't usually go racing off after suspects with some private citizen with a hair-brained theory. If you think it's a mess back there, you should see the paperwork I'll have tomorrow." He snatched a cell phone from his pocket, flipped it open, and called the command post back at the crime scene. "I want you to double-check all the documentation while I'm gone," he said to the officer he had left in control. "You make sure all evidence is accounted for before anyone leaves, you got that? Don't release the scene until I'm back."

Washington clicked the cell phone shut. "Now, tell me," he said to Danny. "If Boyle didn't kill Conway, why did you come to Boyle's house?"

"First of all, the living will that Fintan Conway supposedly signed was forged."

"How do you know?"

"I took it to Tim Peterson. He's a forensic document examiner."

"I know who Tim Peterson is."

"Peterson left a message on my machine. Conway's signature on the living will was not the same as the signature on the other documents I also got from Maureen Conway for verification."

"A guy can get a little shaky when he's signing his life away."

"Then there's this." Danny reached inside the file, removed a printout, and handed it to Washington.

"Am I supposed to read this while I drive? What is it?"

"It's a column Fintan Conway wrote in nineteen ninety-five about a drug dealer Uptown by the name of Tito Rodriguez, who got murdered."

"You're still harping on this Tito character. Lots of drug dealers got their clocks punched Uptown in the 'nineties. Lots of them named Rodriguez, I'm sure."

"Conway took a particular interest in this case."

"Oh, yeah?" Washington cocked his head. "Wasn't it a Kate Rodriguez that Conway was boinking on the side?"

"He wasn't *boinking* anybody," Danny snapped. "He was trying to help somebody out. But I kept wondering why he was so interested in this one case."

Danny peered through the car window at the open maw of the Bronx skyline, its crumbling tenements like rotten teeth. Lights had come on in the apartments, turning the skyline into a checkerboard of dark and light squares of windows. The rain had stopped and a sickle of moon had risen and snagged on a corner of an abandoned project.

In a few minutes, Danny pointed to a row of single-family homes along 217th Street. "Turn here."

As they pulled in front of Fintan Conway's house, Danny could see a light on in the living room. He looked back at the file and saw a scribbled note in the margin of an article. "Mineral rights revert to Don on my death." A window was open and as they got out of the car he could hear the babble of the TV.

"Don't tell me you think Conway's old lady killed him 'cause she was jealous of his young lover," said Washington. "You brought me here to arrest his widow? Come on, O'Flaherty, you can do better than that."

"Just wait. I want to see if we can find the last article Conway wrote."

"We already have it. It came out two days before St. Paddy's Day."

"No, I mean the very last."

When Maureen Conway came to the door, Danny told her that Don Boyle was dead.

"What happened to him?"

"The police found him hanging by his neck at home."

"My God. Suicide?"

Danny started to answer but Washington cut him off. "We're not sure yet."

Danny told her they wanted to see if there was anything on the hard drive of Conway's computer.

Within minutes, Danny and Washington had

printed out Fintan Conway's final column written on a Toshiba laptop that he used at home.

Gold on Croagh Patrick

"By the way," Danny said. "That's pronounced *'Crow* Patrick.'"

"I'll be damned."

March 17. Judas Iscariot sold out Christ for thirty pieces of silver. Some people in Ireland are selling out St. Patrick's holy mountain for a crock of gold. That gold may or may not be at the end of the rainbow.

Traces of gold have been discovered on Croagh Patrick in County Mayo. Long a pilgrimage site for devout Catholics, now it is attracting a far different kind of devotee. Those who worship money.

Real estate speculators, mining companies, geologists, corrupt clerics and greedy landowners all have their eyes on the gold.

St. Patrick would turn over in his grave.

An unusual coalition of environmentalists, truly devout Christians, and locals who deplore the desecration of the mountain, have joined forces to stop the proposed mining.

Washington looked up before he had turned the page. "I still don't get it, O'Flaherty. What is all this supposed to prove?"

"Maureen," Danny said to Mo Conway, "tell Detective Washington about the land in Ireland."

"Don Boyle and my husband were partners in a

land deal in Ireland. Back in 'ninety-three or 'ninety-four when me and Finn and Boyle and his wife were all good friends, we bought a piece of land together at the foot of Croagh Patrick with a ruined cottage on it. At first we were going to build a vacation home that we could all use as a kind of time share. Then the idea was to build separate retirement homes on it. Well, as the years went on, the friendship faded. Finn had something against Don Boyle that I never understood. He never told me why all of a sudden he didn't want to have anything more to do with the Boyles."

"I'll tell you why," Danny interrupted. He held up the file folder. "It's all in here. Boyle had been doing a lot of double-dealing Uptown. He owned two buildings in Washington Heights."

"We knew that."

"One of the buildings was on One Hundred Seventy-eighth Street. When your husband realized that Tito Rodriguez had rented a storefront in that building from Boyle for his bodega he started looking deeper into the death of Rodriguez. He found out that Tito wasn't a drug dealer at all. He was a respectable small businessman who owned several bodegas. It turns out that Boyle had been offered a lot of money by a gang of drug dealers from Miami. The bodega was just off the exit from the GWB. They wanted to use the store as a drop-off spot for drugs. A car could come up from Miami on I-95, drop the shipment and be back on the highway heading south within minutes of arriving in the city. Only problem was that Tito Rodriguez had just signed a two-year lease and had no desire to get involved with drug dealers. So Don Boyle agreed to rent the store to the drug dealers if they could get rid of Tito. So they murdered him and made it look like a drug deal gone bad.''

"My God. I can't believe this," said Mo.

"Boyle needed to launder the cash he got from the deal, so he used it to buy his share of the land in Ireland. He used Fintan and Maureen to make sure the deal looked respectable.''

"I had no idea!''

"Neither did your husband," Danny added. "At least not at first. When he found all this out he was mad enough to kill Boyle himself. But he was too deep into the land deal to do anything about it. It might have been hard to explain to the authorities how he had gotten involved. I suppose he had his reputation as a newspaperman to consider, too. Still, he felt guilty and started giving money to Tito Rodriguez's widow. By then, Fintan and Boyle hated each other.''

"Now it makes sense," said Maureen.

"Not to me," said Washington. "Get to the point, O'Flaherty.''

"Then gold was discovered on Croagh Patrick.''

"The holy mountain, right?''

"Yes. Even before St. Patrick, the Druids considered it a holy mountain and led their followers to the top to seek enlightenment. As far as Christianity, it is documented that a chapel existed there since at least AD eight twenty-four. In eleven-thirteen, thirty fasting pilgrims were struck by lightening and killed on the night of the festival of Patrick. The pope granted them indulgences. Every year thousands of people, even today, make pilgrimages to the mountain, many in bare feet.''

"All right, O'Flaherty, thanks for the history lesson. What's this got to do with Fintan Conway?"

"Well, a couple years ago the Irish government contracted with a geologist and his company to explore the feasibility of extracting gold from the mountain," Danny quoted from the file. "The geologist's company spent considerable up-front money doing just that, then wrangled to recover some of the costs from the government when things started to get messy with the locals who opposed the mining. In the meantime, the media heated up."

"To a lot of people in Ireland," Maureen added, "it didn't seem right that they were desecrating a holy site like that."

"The mining firm had built a service road up the mountain, which the company contended didn't hurt the environment but helped with access," Danny went on. "You know, made it easier for tourists who didn't want to do an actual pilgrimage. It's twenty-five hundred feet to the top of the mountain. Some people aren't *that* devoted to St. Patrick. Anyway, shortly after the start-up of the project, the environmentalists got involved and spread their message to the media, fighting the development."

"Didn't the Catholic Church try to stop the mining?" asked Washington. "Aren't they the guys who call the shots over there?"

"In fact," Danny explained, "the Bishop of Tuam either was silent or tacitly supported the development-or at least in private conversations with the geologist, said it was okay. Later, when things got nasty, the Bishop changed his mind and apparently went on TV making some defamatory remarks about the geologist and his company. Tried to distance himself from the whole thing. The geologist sued the bishop and the station.''

"Christ, you people fight over *everything*,'' Washington put in.

"In the meantime, Don Boyle started getting ideas. He went to Fintan and said why didn't they hire someone to see if there was gold on their property, or at least explore selling the mineral rights.'' Danny paused. "The mineral rights were jointly held. But there was a clause—''

"My husband wanted no part of any of it,'' Maureen interrupted. "He thought it was a shame that everybody was all of a sudden willing to destroy a site that had been considered sacred for centuries, in order to make a profit. He opposed the development and had no interest in making money from his own land. He wanted us to retire there.''

"Not so Boyle,'' Danny added. "He was dying to get his hands on whatever gold might be found on the property, the environment and St. Patrick be damned. He argued with Fintan. Tried to get your husband to change his mind. Boyle told Fintan that if he said anything about what he knew of Tito Rodriguez, he'd implicate Fintan as well. After all, they were partners in the land deal. He could make it look like Fintan was somehow a partner in the murder of Rodriguez, too.''

"My husband never killed anybody,'' said Mo Conway.

"Of course not,'' said Danny. "Besides, Don Boyle had another ace in the hole. The mineral rights reverted to him on your husband's death.''

"What?''

"That's right, Mo. He didn't even need your approval to extract gold or sell the rights once Finn was out of the way."

"My God."

"I get it," said Washington. "When Conway said he didn't want mining done on the land, Boyle was ready to kill him. Then to add insult to injury, Conway was about to publish an article condemning the desecration of St. Patrick's holy mountain. Maybe he figured Conway would mention him somehow. Besides that, Boyle needed to make sure no one ever found out about who murdered Tito Rodriguez. So, somebody dressed up in a mask on St. Paddy's Day and shot Fintan Conway. Boyle called in a tip to Crimestoppers Hotline and set up this guy Brendan to make it look political. Then Boyle hung himself because he knew he'd never get away with it."

Danny smiled. "Close, but no cigar. First of all, Ian Masters was the one who called Crimestoppers Hotline."

"That's the guy in the band, right?"

"Right. Boyle paid him five thousand dollars to phone in an anonymous tip."

"Okay," said Washington.

"So Boyle has a motive, but no opportunity. As you know, he was sitting on the reviewing stand in plain sight of hundreds of people when Fintan Conway was shot. Don Boyle didn't kill him."

"You're wasting my time, O'Flaherty. Get to the point."

"We've got one more house call to make," said Danny.

THIRTY

DETECTIVE WASHINGTON double-parked in front of Kate Rodriguez's apartment building and Danny jumped out. The rain had begun again and quickly turned to hail. Marbles of ice clattered on the hood of the unmarked police car.

The building was a 21-story housing project on the upper west tip of Manhattan. Built in 1960, the rusty brick exterior had the look of former Soviet Bloc architecture.

"If you think Conway's sweetie murdered him, what's all this stuff about gold on some holy mountain?" asked Washington as they approached the front door of Kate's building. "The only gold digger in this case is your friend Kate."

"She's no gold digger."

"And what about this living will? You never said who forged it."

"Boyle forged it. He was thinking all along that if his first plan didn't work, and Conway somehow survived the attack, he wanted to make sure he died one way or another. I'm not sure how he did it yet, but I also got a sample of Boyle's handwriting and the document examiner verified that it was probably Boyle who forged the living will."

"That's cold, man. But I thought you said Boyle didn't kill anybody."

"He didn't pull the trigger himself."

A young woman with a baby stroller exited the front door of the apartment building and Danny and Detective Washington entered the lobby without being buzzed in. They took the elevator and got out on the 9th floor. A narrow hall painted an institutional green led to apartment 9-C.

"Danny!" Kate Rodriguez said in surprise as she opened the door to her apartment.

"Hello, Kate."

"What are you doing here?"

"This is Detective Washington of the NYPD."

"I know who he is," said Kate. "If you're here about Fintan Conway, I don't know anything more than I've already told you."

"May we come in?" Danny asked.

"Why not?"

Danny and Detective Washington stepped into the foyer of Kate's small two-bedroom apartment. The foyer led straight ahead to a cluttered kitchen piled with dirty dishes, and to the left to a living room littered with toys and a blasting TV, unwatched, in a corner.

"Sorry for the mess," she apologized. Her two daughters fought over a palm-sized Nintendo game on the living room floor. "Stop it!"

They ignored her. Kate heaved a weary sigh and pushed a loose strand of hair out of her face. "I'd offer you something, but I haven't shopped in..."

"Don't worry about it, Kate," said Danny. "Listen, I brought Detective Washington here because I think I know now why Fintan Conway was giving you money over the years. And why he put you in his will.''

"Let's sit down here," she said, pointing to the kitchen table squeezed into a corner of the foyer. The table was piled with mail, videos, toys, and newspapers.

"I think Fintan Conway found out who murdered your husband.''

"This is all speculation, O'Flaherty," Washington added hastily.

"He was murdered by drug dealers," said Kate. "But my husband was no drug dealer. Nobody ever investigated because he was Hispanic.''

Washington, who should have risen to the defense of the NYPD, was silent.

"They just figured another dead Dominican dope dealer," Kate went on bitterly. "But he never had anything to do with drugs. He hated drugs.''

Danny explained Don Boyle's connection to Fintan Conway, the land in Ireland, and what Conway had found out about the murder of Kate's husband.

"You're telling me Fintan Conway knew who killed my husband?" Kate said angrily after she heard the story. "And he did nothing about it. Wrote one lousy column." Her voice shook. "Why didn't he go to the police?''

"I think he was afraid that since he was a business partner of Boyle, it would look bad for him. So he did the only thing he could think of. He sent you money, then put you in his will.''

"But what about this Irish guy who was accused of killing him?''

"He got set up. Don Boyle gave this guy named

Ian Masters, the singer in Brendan Grady's band, five thousand dollars to call in an anonymous tip to the police."

"He framed this poor Irish guy?"

"That's right. Boyle even put word out through his connections with various paramilitary organizations that the Red Hand Brigade was going to hit Fintan Conway at the parade. That's how Brendan and ARM got lured into the Plaza Hotel on St. Patrick's Day. Boyle muddied the waters as much as he could. ARM thought they were going to stop the Red Hand from killing Conway."

"You're saying that was all set up by one man—Don Boyle?" Kate asked.

"That's right. He set up an elaborate plan for a murder. But he didn't carry out the murder himself. That was the genius of his scheme. Instead, he led someone to believe that the murder of Tito Rodriguez was really Fintan Conway's doing, didn't he, Kate?"

"What are you talking about?"

"He led someone to believe it was Fintan Conway who had murdered your husband. Then that someone put on a mask on St. Patrick's Day and shot Conway to avenge Tito Rodriguez's death."

"You're crazy." Kate Rodriguez looked around with wide eyes, her chest heaving. "I don't know what you're talking about."

"Then that certain someone realized Fintan Conway did *not* murder Tito Rodriguez and instead went hunting for Don Boyle. Found him in his apartment and murdered him."

"Stop it!" Kate screamed.

One of the children in the other room started crying. "What's wrong, Mommy?" The child stepped into the kitchen dragging a Pooh Bear hung by a cord around its neck.

This was the hardest thing Danny had ever done in his life. "Where is he, Kate?"

"What?"

"Where is he?"

Just then the locks on the door rattled and Joey opened it. He looked quickly at his mother, then Detective Washington, then Danny.

Joey bolted down the hall.

THIRTY-ONE

DANNY AND WASHINGTON raced out the door.

"Joey!" Danny yelled.

His voice echoed in the empty hallway as he and the detective ran to the elevator. When Danny and Washington reached the lobby, Joey had already dashed through the front door. They saw him leap down the outside stairs, knocking over a young woman carrying two bags of groceries. Joey ran into the street.

"Come back!"

"Damn kids," the woman muttered as she scrambled to her feet and tried to gather her spilled groceries. "They're ruining this neighborhood."

Joey dashed across the street and Danny sprinted after him into the path of a car.

"Watch where you're going," the driver screamed out the window at Danny.

Detective Washington ran to his car to radio for backup, then swung the car into the street and took off after Joey.

Danny chased Joey down the sidewalk, then Joey turned abruptly and disappeared down an alley between buildings. Danny raced into the dark alley, tripped over a garbage can, and went sailing. When he picked himself up his hands bled from breaking his fall on the cement. He saw Joey scale a chain-link fence at the back of the alley that separated the trash-filled courtyard behind the building from the court-yard of the next building.

Joey was nearly to the top of the fence when Danny caught up with him, reached up and grabbed him by the foot. Joey twisted his leg back and forth and wrenched free of Danny's grasp. As Danny stood holding Joey's empty sneaker in one hand, the boy pulled himself to the top of the fence and vaulted into the courtyard of the next building, then hobbled down the alley of that building.

"Joey, stop," Danny yelled through the fence. "Let me help you."

Danny scaled the fence, snagged his pants on the top, and ripped the seat out of them as he dropped to the ground on the other side and raced across the courtyard. He could hear sirens in the distance, draw-ing closer.

When Danny came out of the alley, he saw Joey run through the front door of an apartment building just as an elderly man exited. Danny ran to the door but it had already closed and he was locked out. He reached up and put both hands over the panel of but-tons that rang the buzzers of each apartment. He pushed hard, buzzing twenty different apartments si-multaneously. Immediately, someone buzzed him in and he ran into the building and up the stairs.

Joey must know someone here, Danny thought as he climbed the stairs. If he was already inside an apartment, Danny would never find him. He kept climbing the stairs, looking at the closed door of each apartment. He'd have to knock at each one. What good would that do him? If Joey was hiding in a friend's house, they'd just say he wasn't there.

When Danny reached the fifth floor, he started to run back down the stairs when he remembered the roof. He climbed two more flights of stairs and pushed on the door to the roof; it was open.

As soon as Danny came out onto the tar and gravel roof, he spotted a human form crouched in a dark corner.

"Joey, please," Danny said to him. "You're only making it worse. Give yourself up."

Joey leapt from his crouched position and climbed the waist-high wall enclosing the roof. Between this building and the next was a space of about fifteen feet, six stories above the alley where garbage from the apartment building was piled.

"Joey, no," Danny screamed.

Just as Danny yelled "no," Joey was airborn.

It seemed to Danny that minutes passed as Joey sailed between the two buildings. The tail of his shirt trailed behind him as he led with his bare foot. Danny couldn't believe what he was watching. Joey fell short and hit the wall of the opposite building with a thud. But as he slid down the side of the building one hand snagged the top of the wall and he clung to it. Panting and grunting, he heaved his other arm over the wall. Joey hung there, six stories above the street, his forearms on the top of the wall. Danny could see his chest rise and fall rapidly as he struggled for air. Joey rested a moment, then scrambled with his feet to get a toehold. But the foot without a sneaker kept slipping on the side of the building.

Danny heard a shrill siren and looked down into the street. Three squad cars with red lights flashing parked in front of the building. A lone officer ran into the alley, looked up and shouted, "Up there." He spoke into the radio microphone clipped to his lapel and two other officers ran into the alley.

Joey got the toe of his sneaker into a chink in the brick wall and heaved himself up, throwing his shoeless foot over the wall.

A chopper whirred over the Harlem River and scissored the rooftops with twin searchlights.

Within seconds, Joey had scrambled onto the other roof.

Danny heaved a sigh of relief that Joey had made it. Then, before he even had time to think about it, Danny backed up, took a running leap over the wall, and vaulted across the space between buildings. He hit the top of the wall with his shins, flipped and rolled across the gravel roof. He could barely stand from the pain in his shins, but he managed to rise and chase after Joey. "Let me help you," he yelled.

Joey dashed to the back of the roof and clambered down the iron fire escape. Danny climbed down after him. Where were the cops? Danny wondered as Joey dropped into the courtyard behind the building and ran to the chain-link fence, climbed over it, and jumped into the adjoining apartment's alley. Danny scaled the fence and chased Joey down the alleyway.

When Danny came out of the alley into the street, Joey stood against Washington's car in the freezing rain, his hands on the roof, his legs spread, panting heavily.

"You have the right to remain silent. Anything you say can and will be used against you in a court of law."

Squad cars bounced red balls of light across the

buildings and police radios crackled with orders. A half dozen car alarms barked in the street like rabid dogs. The helicopter he had seen earlier swooped overhead, raking the street with light.

Danny could not bear to watch or listen to Washington reading his student the Miranda Warning.

"You have the right to speak to an attorney, and to have an attorney present during any questioning."

The detective's voice droned in the background as two more backup units arrived with sirens squawking. "If you cannot afford a lawyer, one will be provided for you..."

As Danny walked down the block away from the police, he did something he had not done in a long time. He prayed.

Danny O'Flaherty prayed for the soul of Joey Rodriguez.

THIRTY-TWO

DANNY STAYED SEQUESTERED in his apartment all day Saturday, ordering Chinese food and pizza, and catching up on neglected schoolwork.

His shins were badly bruised and his hands throbbed from where he'd scraped them during the chase. On top of that, he'd caught a cold and he felt woozy and worn out. But most of all he was depressed about Joey. It wasn't the hoods under the subway tracks who had gotten him into trouble, after all. It was Don Boyle who had turned the boy into a murderer.

Detective Washington called to tell him that they had booked Joey Rodriguez at the 19th Precinct station house and he was taken downtown the next morning to the Criminal Courts Building at 100 Centre Street for arraignment. His mother had hired an attorney and hoped she'd be able to pledge the coming inheritance from Fintan Conway as bail.

But the judge thought that given his fondness for running, Joey might flee again, so he denied bail. Then Joey was taken to Rikers to wait for his day in court.

Danny wondered how Joey would survive among the other, older inmates. He shuddered to think of

Joey in there. It was weird that Brendan was free from that place and Joey was now a prisoner.

Detective Washington told Danny that Joey would be facing murder charges for both Boyle and Conway.

Danny spoke to Fidelma on the phone Saturday night. She wanted to come over and feed him chicken soup, but Danny needed to be alone. They agreed to meet after school on Tuesday, April 3rd at Coogan's for dinner. Danny called Detective Washington and invited him to come along. He wanted to find out everything he could about Joey.

When Danny finally went downstairs Sunday morning, it was one of those days that come as a surprise in early April, when Danny assumed that the worst of winter was behind them. When he stepped into the street and looked down 207th, snow blew at an angle nearly perpendicular to the ground. The cars parked along the street were dusted white. The few people outside clutched their coats around them as they struggled against the blowing snow. Danny made his way to the bodega across from his apartment and bought a copy of the Daily News. Silvio, the guy behind the counter who usually never gave him the time of day, handed two papers to Danny and waved away his money.

The headlines made Danny shudder:

STUDENT HELD IN SLAYING OF GRAND MARSHAL
TEACHER HELPS NAB SUSPECT

April 1, 2001. A senior at John F. Kennedy High School in the Bronx was arrested Friday night and charged in a brutal double murder.

The student's first victim, Fintan Patrick Conway, the grand marshal of this year's St. Patrick's Day parade was gunned down, police say, by eighteen-year-old Joseph Sean Rodriguez. Police claim the student used a small-caliber pistol with a silencer to pump three bullets into his victim. Conway died at St. Luke's-Roosevelt Hospital four days after the attack from gunshot wounds to the lungs and chest.

The youth has also been charged with murder in the first degree in connection with the death of Donald Boyle. The victim was found hanging from the neck by a lamp cord in his Bronx apartment on Friday, March 30th.

Police were led to the youth's uptown apartment, where he lives with his mother and two sisters, by a teacher at Kennedy High School—Daniel O'Flaherty. Investigators are still attempting to unravel the bizarre chain of events that led to the murders of both...

Danny could not force himself to read the rest of the article.

On Monday morning, April 2nd, Danny made an appointment to see an old friend of his father, Moishe Finkelstein. Moishe agreed to meet Danny after school at his shop in the heart of New York's diamond district. Although Moishe did not really run a retail shop, Danny knew he would fix him up with something special at a reasonable price.

The entrance of Moishe's shop on West 48th Street sat between a bagel shop and an off-track betting office. Danny signed in with security and walked to the elevator. A surveillance camera overhead followed

Danny as he pushed the button for the 4th floor and stepped inside the elevator. A young couple filed in behind him, and as soon as the elevator doors closed they fell on each other hungrily.

Danny stepped out onto the fourth floor, and had trouble finding the door he was looking for. He had only been here one time, years ago, with his father. Certainly nothing fancy here, and definitely nothing to indicate that millions of dollars worth of diamonds were changing hands behind these doors. Finally he spotted a small sign for Moishe Finkelstein and a sign that read: Protected by Alarm System. Danny pushed the buzzer.

"Yes."

"Danny O'Flaherty. Here to see Mr. Finkelstein."

The outer door clicked and Danny pushed it open to be faced with yet another door that would not open until he had stepped into the narrow passage and closed the first. Then the second door buzzed and Danny stepped inside. It was a nondescript office with a frayed gray carpet on the floor and a picture of Rabbi Schneerson, the old Hasidic holy man believed by followers to be the messiah, on the wall.

The Indian receptionist was busy at a computer. "Have a seat, sir," she said in her lovely accent. "Mr. Finkelstein will be right with you."

Danny sat down and looked around the office. Behind the receptionist was a large safe. The walls were adorned with mounted certificates in Hebrew. They looked like either diplomas or some kind of professional certifications.

Ten minutes later, Moishe entered the office from a back room and extended his ringed hand. "Danny.

You look wonderful. The last time I saw you... well, it was many years ago."

Moishe was in his seventies but looked much younger with a neat mustache, closely cropped graying hair, crisp white shirt with diamond cuff links, a diamond stickpin in his crimson tie, and a yarmulke on his head.

They sat down at a white formica-topped table. "Now," he said, standing up almost immediately. "I have a few things in your price range." He kept his tone objective with no hint whatsoever that the price Danny had mentioned on the phone was probably as low as he went. Clearly, Mr. Finkelstein was doing Danny a favor.

He disappeared for a moment, then returned with four cloth cases that he set on the table. He took the first case, snapped off the velcro and opened the four overlapping sides that were folded like a blanket. Inside were four pockets, each containing diamond rings.

"I've read all about you in the newspaper," said Moishe.

"Yeah," Danny said without enthusiasm. "It's been a pretty crazy couple of weeks."

Moishe let the loupe he was gripping between his eyelids fall to the cloth case and looked at Danny. "Your mother and father would be so happy."

"You mean about helping catch the murderer?"

Moishe laughed. "No, no." He nodded to the display of rings.

Danny smiled. "Yes. They would."

After he'd seen some of the rings, Danny asked to see more, and Moishe disappeared into the back room again.

The moment Danny saw the two-caret diamond set in its platinum band, he knew it was the one he wanted. "I'll take it," he said, reaching inside his coat pocket for his checkbook.

After they closed the deal, Moishe Finkelstein said, "One time your father and I had a long talk about our children."

"Oh, really?"

"Yes. I told him that my oldest boy, Abe, was not going to become a diamond dealer. I was very disappointed. He had decided to become a teacher."

"I didn't know that."

"Yes. He teaches high school in Queens."

"I had no idea," said Danny.

"You know what your father said when I told him how Abe had let me down?"

"I guess he told you he was pretty disappointed that I didn't become an undertaker."

"Yes, he did say that."

Danny folded his hands in his lap like a student who'd been reprimanded.

"But then he said, 'My son became a teacher and I am so proud of him. What have I done with my life, Moishe? Bury dead people? Their lives are over when I see them. My son works with the living whose lives have just begun. He can really make a difference. I'm glad he didn't listen to me. He's a great teacher.'"

"Dad said that?" A lump had formed in Danny's throat.

"Yes, he did."

Danny swallowed hard, not sure what to say.

"Good luck," said Moishe. "And congratulations."

THIRTY-THREE

SOME EVENTS IN LIFE change a person forever. Later, one looks back on these events from the perspective of a new and different individual. Sometimes a better one; sometimes worse. But always older and maybe wiser. The death of Danny's last parent was one of these events. When his father had died four years before, Danny realized at that moment that he was not only an orphan now, but he had ceased to be a child forever.

The capture of Joey Rodriguez, and his subsequent arrest for the murder of Fintan Conway and Donald Boyle, was another life-changing event in Danny's life. Never had he felt so disappointed in being unable to stop what had happened. Never had he felt so powerless. He had wanted to save Joey from a life on the streets. But he was too late. Now a life on the streets did not seem so bad to Danny. Joey faced a life in prison—maybe death row.

Even though he should have been relieved it was all over with at last, Danny found no satisfaction in finding Fintan Conway's murderer. On the contrary, he wished he had never gotten involved in the whole mess to begin with. Brendan Grady was a fugitive, Joey Rodriguez was in jail, and Conway and Boyle were dead.

What your deed is, so is your destiny.

The snow had melted quickly overnight and a brilliant sun shone, toasting the streets of Manhattan. It was a beautiful Tuesday, April 3rd—warm and clear. Danny heard the *thunk* of tennis balls, the cries of children. Office workers in business suits and sneakers walked smiling, their coats open or slung over their shoulders. The freshly raked clay infield of a baseball diamond smelled like a spring garden ready to be planted. It had been exactly sixteen days since the murder of Fintan Conway.

Outside Coogan's, a tennis shoe dangled from the branch of a withered tree and cassette tapes hung like ornaments from its pathetic branches. Danny paused to notice a swollen bud, its green insides already visible, ready to burst into leaf on this mockery of a tree.

Spring was on its way.

Danny joined Fidelma Muldoon and Detective Washington at a table in the back of the bar. Washington ate his catsup-smothered hamburger deluxe in silence. Danny sipped a pint of Harp Lager and picked at his fish and chips. Fidelma fiddled with a Greek salad.

"What are Joey's chances?" Danny asked, finally.

"Not good," said Washington. "I'm sure the judge will take into consideration that Boyle was responsible for the death of Joey's father. But Joey's facing murder one for Fintan Conway, too. He's going to be doing some long, hard time, but I'm sure he won't get the hot shot."

"The poor child," said Fidelma.

"He's not a child," said Washington. "Rodriguez turned eighteen on March first and he'll be tried as an adult. Besides, there are ten-year-olds out there who'd put a bullet in your brain pan for the change in your pockets. So, please don't waste your pity on the children," Washington said. "Penny for your thoughts, O'Flaherty." He put a French fry in his mouth.

Danny took a sip of his Harp and ran his finger around the rim of the glass. "I just wish I could have seen what was happening with Joey and stopped him."

"We'd all like a crystal ball, O'Flaherty." Washington slurped his coffee. "But life don't work that way."

"Don't blame yourself, Danny," Fidelma soothed. But Danny did blame himself.

"I still don't understand how Joey's father fits into this," Fidelma said.

"The father rented a storefront at the foot of the George Washington Bridge. He had a little grocery store, a bodega," Washington explained. "These drug dealers from Miami wanted to use the store as a drop-off point for their shipments. They could get off I-95 and be in and out of the city in minutes. They went to Tito Rodriguez and offered him a deal. He refused. So they went to the owner of the building, Donald Boyle. He was more than happy to accommodate them. They offered him ten times the rent he was getting from Tito Rodriguez, plus twenty-five thousand. Boyle's only problem was the two-year lease Tito had just signed. 'Leave it to us,' the drug dealers told him. They said they'd make sure the tenant got out of the store as long as Boyle agreed to rent it to them as soon as it was empty."

"So, Boyle didn't actually kill Joey's father," said Fidelma.

"Oh, no. Boyle didn't pull the trigger himself."

"The drug dealers murdered him," Danny added. "Made it look like a drug deal gone bad. Boyle made all kinds of statements to the cops about how he was sick of people like Tito Rodriguez screwing up the neighborhood. Now he had a good clean tenant who wanted to open a laundry there. The Miami boys had a front man who was sparkling clean and they put a laudromat in."

Washington smiled. "A laundromat. Nice touch there, huh?"

"But how did Joey figure out that it was really Boyle who was responsible for his father's death?" Fidelma asked.

"He hasn't told us that yet. But we do know that Boyle was a real sicko." Washington picked up another French fry. "A greedy sicko. When Joey found out how his father really died, he confronted Boyle with the truth. Boyle manipulated the poor kid into thinking it was really Fintan Conway who had killed his father. He even gave the kid the mask and a gun equipped with a silencer. It all came out in the kid's confession. Then when we searched Joey's room, we found the murder weapon and silencer and traced them back to Boyle. We had another talk with Ian Masters, too. He admitted that Don Boyle paid him five thousand to call in a phony tip. I'm afraid Mr. Masters' music career's going to be on hold for awhile."

"Joey's poor mother is devastated," Danny said.

"We still don't know how much she knew."

"Come on," said Danny. "She had no idea. And I still can't believe it was Joey. He didn't seem like the kind of kid who would want to avenge his father's death."

"You never know. Boyle manipulated the kid. Told him a bunch of lies about his father and his mother and Finn Conway. Made it sound like she and Conway were responsible for his dad's death. We also found out Boyle was probably skimming money from parade funds over the years." Washington ate the last of his French fries and stood up. "I've gotta run."

"One more thing," Danny said. "What about that hotel room at the Plaza? What actually did go on there?"

"Nothing," said Washington, "and everything. All Boyle wanted was to get Brendan Grady up there and get his fingerprints in the room."

"I thought a tourist from Holland was registered in the room?"

"He was, compliments of Boyle. Apparently, Boyle posed as some kind of a salesman. Met this tourist near Times Square and awarded him a free couple of nights at the Plaza. Gave the guy cash to pay for the room and got an extra key. When the tourist was out sightseeing or whatever, Boyle left spent shell casings in the room."

"He was certainly thorough," said Danny.

"Thoroughly nuts," said Washington. "Then Boyle put out the word that the Red Hand Brigade was going to hit Fintan Conway at the St. Patrick's Day parade from this Dutch tourist's hotel room. He made it sound as though the Red Hand was going to blame ARM for the shooting. The poor schmuck from Holland was probably out touring the Statue of Liberty while this was all going on. We interviewed him later. Totally clueless."

"It was all a hoax to lure ARM into the room," Danny added.

"That's right. ARM sends Brendan in there to try to prevent the murder. Meanwhile, Boyle has Ian Masters phone in his tip to Crimestoppers Hotline. Cops race up to the Plaza to find the gunman. But Joey Rodriguez is on the ground with the mask and gun Boyle gave him. Shoots the grand marshal. Cops find the hotel room empty but they pick up Brendan at the pub nearby. ARM thought they'd been double-crossed by the Red Hand Brigade. Joey, meanwhile, takes off the mask and disappears into the crowd."

"The only problem," Danny added, "is that Joey Rodriguez is smarter than Boyle thought he was. Joey figured out he'd been used and he turned on Don Boyle."

"That's about it." The detective extended his hand to Danny. "Thanks, O'Flaherty. I'm sorry I doubted you. You ought to get a medal. I mean that. I brought it up to the police commissioner this morning."

"I don't want any medals," Danny said bitterly. "I hate the way this thing turned out."

"That's the real world, O'Flaherty. Murder is a messy business. Like I said, we don't gather the suspects..."

"... in the library at the end of the day and announce who done it," Danny said wearily. "I know, I know."

"But you were right," Washington added. "It's not just forensics. It is about stories, too."

Danny shook the detective's hand. "It's been a pleasure."

"Good luck to you, O'Flaherty."

"Thanks."

"By the way, what about those guys in the" —Washington smiled—"Calypso green C280 Mercedes?"

Danny glanced at Fidelma, then back at Washington. "What about them?"

"Who were they?"

Danny winked at Fidelma. "I don't know."

Washington left the restaurant, after giving them both a raised eyebrow, letting them know he knew he was being conned.

Danny and Fidelma finished their food and ordered another round of drinks. Danny had been doing a lot of thinking since Joey's arrest two days ago.

"What do you think happened to Brendan?" Danny asked. He'd been almost as worried about Brendan *after* he'd escaped as he had been when he was in jail.

"He's safe," said Fidelma.

"How can you be sure?"

"I called his parents again, and they told me that ARM had gotten a message to them."

"Where is he?"

"They wouldn't say. In hiding. But they assured me he was fine, or at least that's what the ARM people said. They also told me there's a proposal on the table in Stormont for asylum for all political fugitives, so he may come home sooner than anybody expected."

All that weekend Danny had turned over in his mind the events of the last couple weeks. He was not getting any younger and it was time to settle a few issues in his own life. Maybe it wasn't the best time or place to bring it up, but Danny had something important to ask Fidelma.

Fidelma watched him intently, her eyes searching his face. Sensing that he wanted to talk, she said, "What is it, Danny?"

You are your deepest driving desire.

"There's something I've been wanting to talk to you about."

"Yes?"

He glanced around, then reached into his coat pocket and took out the tiny case, opened it, and handed it to Fidelma.

She looked at the diamond engagement ring sparkling in its velvet-lined box. "Fidelma," Danny said. "Will you marry me?"

She did not seem surprised by the question, but she declined to answer it. "Let me sleep on it."

"Fidelma, that's no answer."

"You've waited forty-three years to get married. You can wait another twenty-four hours."

Danny sat back and examined her, then smiled. He snapped the case shut and put it in his coat pocket. "Okay. Sleep on it. But I want an answer tomorrow."

"You'll have one."

"You know," Danny said, still unable to get his mind off the murder even after proposing marriage to the woman he loved. "Conway wrote something like two thousand columns in his professional career."

"That's a lot of stories," said Fidelma.

"Yes, it is." Danny took a sip of his pint. "I was just thinking. I guess as far as Fintan Conway's story goes...this is it."

"This is what?" Fidelma asked.

Danny smiled over the rim of his glass. "The end."

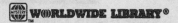

Lost in Austin

A Tony Kozol Mystery

When a broken arm sidelines the guitarist for a popular country band, struggling musician Tony Kozol gets a gig as the temporary replacement. But when the band arrives in Austin for a week at the Southwest Music Conference—murder takes center stage.

The victim was a roadie with the group, and Tony soon spots an unsettling connection to the band—especially when the body of a pretty young groupie is found next. Sounds to Tony like a song in the making: a tale full of heartbreak and woe, longing and desire. It could be a hit. That is, if he lives long enough to write it.

J. R. Ripley

"J. R. Ripley continues
to delight."
—*Midwest Book Review*

Available April 2002
at your favorite retail outlet.

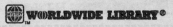

Take 2 books and a surprise gift FREE!

SPECIAL LIMITED-TIME OFFER

MEMORIES CAN BE MURDER

A Charlie Parker Mystery

CONNIE SHELTON

While stowing boxes away in her attic, Albuquerque CPA Charlie Parker uncovers chilling information about her father—and his work as a scientist during the Cold War years. Worse, she now suspects the fatal plane crash that killed both her parents was murder.

Determined to solve the fifteen-year-old crime, Charlie quickly learns that asking questions is dangerous. Soon dead ends—and dead bodies—have her worried she's next on the hit list. But what secret is worth killing for after all this time?

"Charlie is slick, appealing, and nobody's fool—just what readers want in an amateur sleuth."
—*Booklist*

Available March 2002 at your favorite retail outlet.

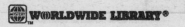

WORLDWIDE LIBRARY®   WCS414